jFIC F628gh
Fleischman Sid 192
The ghost in the noonday
sun,
ESLC90

W9-BXQ-640

DATE DUE

DATE DUE
8 28 89

DATE DUE
D 11 26 91

DUE
9.0

R01247 19240

THE GHOST
IN THE
NOONDAY
SUN

ALSO BY SID FLEISCHMAN

By the Great Horn Spoon!
Chancy and the Grand Rascal
The Ghost on Saturday Night
The Hey Hey Man
Humbug Mountain
Jim Bridger's Alarm Clock
Jingo Django
Longbeard the Wizard
Me and the Man on the Moon-Eyed Horse
Mr. Mysterious & Company
Mr. Mysterious's Secrets of Magic
The Scarebird
The Whipping Boy
The Wooden Cat Man

THE McBROOM BOOKS
McBroom and the Beanstalk
McBroom and the Big Wind
McBroom and the Great Race
McBroom Tells a Lie
McBroom Tells the Truth
McBroom the Rainmaker
McBroom's Almanac
McBroom's Ear
McBroom's Ghost
McBroom's Zoo

Sid Fleischman

THE GHOST IN THE NOONDAY SUN

ILLUSTRATIONS BY PETER SIS

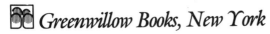 *Greenwillow Books, New York*

DENVER
PUBLIC LIBRARY

JUN ◄◄ 1989

CITY & COUNTY OF DENVER

R01247 19240

Text copyright © 1965 by Albert S. Fleischman
Illustrations copyright © 1989 by Peter Sis
First published as An Atlantic Monthly Press book
by Little, Brown & Co. in 1965
New edition published by Greenwillow Books in 1989
All rights reserved. No part of this book
may be reproduced or utilized in any form
or by any means, electronic or mechanical,
including photocopying, recording or by
any information storage and retrieval
system, without permission in writing
from the Publisher, Greenwillow Books,
a division of William Morrow & Company, Inc.,
105 Madison Avenue, New York, N.Y. 10016.
Printed in the United States of America

10 9 8 7 6 5 4 3 2 1

Library of Congress Cataloging-in-Publication Data

Fleischman, Sid (date)
The ghost in the noonday sun.

Summary: Twelve-year-old Oliver tries to escape
from pirates who take him to an island to find
the ghost and treasure of Gentleman Jack.
    [1. Pirates—Fiction.
2. Buried treasure—Fiction]
I. Title.
PZ7.F5992Gh 1989   [Fic]   88-11066
ISBN 0-688-08140-9

For my mother
For my father

CHAPTERS

THE GHOST
IN THE
NOONDAY
SUN

CHAPTER 1

*In which the wind is howling
and through the door
comes Captain Scratch,
a villain if I ever saw one*

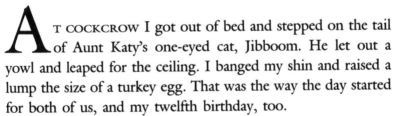

AT COCKCROW I got out of bed and stepped on the tail of Aunt Katy's one-eyed cat, Jibboom. He let out a yowl and leaped for the ceiling. I banged my shin and raised a lump the size of a turkey egg. That was the way the day started for both of us, and my twelfth birthday, too.

After I finished hopping about on one leg I shucked my nightshirt and pulled on my breeches and wool shirt. The water in my pitcher had frozen in the night, so I didn't bother washing my face. I dug out my father's old spyglass.

I leaned through the window, spying out every whaling ship in the harbor. My father was master of the square-rigged *Capricorn*. It had been almost three years since he had put out from Nantucket to hunt whales in the far seas. He was bound to be steering for home now—maybe he'd drop anchor in time for my birthday. But the *Capricorn* was nowhere in sight. There was nothing riding in from the sea but an icy wind to set the shutters banging.

My spyglass stopped at a scurvy-looking ship I had never seen before in Nantucket harbor. She seemed to be neither a whaler nor a trading ship. She was as scarred and tattered as an old fighting cock, and not much larger. One topmast was snapped off and her ratlines were as slack as cobwebs. She rode high in the water, exposing a hull mangy with barnacles and sea grass.

As she swung around on her anchor chain I could make out her name across the stern—the *Sweet Molly*. That seemed a contrary name for such a beggarly ship. Even as I watched she lowered a boat and her captain started ashore. He wore a beaver hat and a greatcoat. The wind whipped his red beard so fiercely that his face looked kindled into flames.

I shut the window to keep out the cold. Of course, the day was just beginning, I told myself, and there was plenty of time for the *Capricorn* to heave in sight.

I went downstairs and Aunt Katy had breakfast waiting for me in the kitchen. She gave me a plump and jolly smile.

"Well, Oliver Finch," she said. Jibboom was winding around her skirts and giving me a wrathy eye. "How does it feel to be twelve years old?"

"Mortal painful," I said. "Especially around my left shin."

We could hear the lodgers begin to stir upstairs and soon they'd be trooping into the public room for breakfast. Aunt Katy was proprietor of the Harpooner's Inn. Her cod chowder was famous among whaling men.

"Aunt Katy," I said. "There's no sign of the *Capricorn* yet."

"It won't be long now. I can feel it in my bones."

"Today, I'm thinking."

She gave a little shrug. "We can't expect thy father to go whaling with a harpoon in one hand and a calendar in the other, can we, dearlove? But mark my word. He's bound for Nantucket this very minute. Did thee wash?"

"The pitcher froze solid," I said.

"Mercy," she laughed. "If I left it to thee, thy ears wouldn't get washed until spring thaw."

She took a kettle from the fireplace and I fetched the soap and pan. After breakfast she told me that old Mr. Wicks, the cooper, had offered to take me on as an apprentice. I told her I didn't take a fancy to making whale-oil barrels as a calling, and she said she didn't take a fancy to my chasing whale spouts through the heathen seas and cannibal isles of the globe. I said that nothing would suit me more. She said nothing would suit her less. I said my father would settle the matter when he got home and he wouldn't have me go a-coopering. She said here's a bit of something for your birthday, Oliver Finch. It was a jackknife with four blades.

There were ships making ready for sea and others rolling out great hogsheads of whale oil. Bowsprits were run up along the wharves like lances. I shied about, looking over the painted figureheads. Those wooden eyes had seen all manner of strange seas. I envied them. I had never been five miles from home. By thunder, I was twelve now, and that was mortal old. Monstrous old. Maybe my father would take me along on his next voyage. But I'd tar myself a pigtail and run off to sea before I let Aunt Katy apprentice me to a landlubber. Yes, sir!

I kept an eye out for the *Capricorn* and exercised my new jackknife on a broken barrel stave. I wore the stave down to a toothpick and then picked my teeth. The afternoon stretched before me—plenty of time for my father to make it. I sat at the end of the wharf and waited. Why, half my friends were at sea and Will Touchwood had been clear to China and back. I felt a powerful yearning to go enterprising after the great whale and see the world for myself.

The light began to fail. My friend Jack Crick, the harpooner, let me climb into the crow's nest of the *Jonas' Revenge*. I kept my eyes peeled for a rag of sail on the horizon. From up there I fancied I could see almost to Africa. I'd be the first to sing out when the *Capricorn* hove into view.

Even after it fell dark I stayed aloft. The wind was a whistler. It shot through my canvas breeches and began whapping over empty barrels below. I was frozen to a stick. I had to put my fingers in my mouth to thaw them out before I could climb down the ratlines. I remembered my father telling me once he had spent winter days in the hot latitudes where if you weren't quick about it a dipper of water would boil before you could get it to your lips. I think he was putting it on some.

All was snug and warm in the public room. I kept the fire blazing in the grate. By then I knew the *Capricorn* wouldn't make port, and I was hugely disappointed.

Aunt Katy's chowder was cooking in the pot and the room began filling up with seafaring men, mostly. Old Mr. Wicks was there in a corner with his arms folded around his stomach.

Aunt Katy let it be known that it was my birthday and

soon Jack Crick was doing an Irish clog by way of merriment. The room got jolly and noisy, except for old Mr. Wicks, who just sat there in the corner. His eyes followed me wherever I went.

And Jibboom was watching me too. There was no love lost between that cat and me. He was up on a crossbeam, silent as a catamount in a tree waiting to pounce on me. His fur was whitish in color, but yellowish too, like old teeth. My father had fetched him up off the jibboom of a wreck in the Pacific islands and brought him home. He must have been a hundred years old, if that were possible—at least, he was on his ninth life for sure. I didn't trust him any more than I'd trust a hungry catamount, either. He was always tracking me. It wouldn't surprise me if that cat had had his bringing up with cannibals.

Aunt Katy was serving up the cod chowder when the door flew open. I thought for a moment it was the wind and the rain. The laughter in the room broke off. Jibboom's fur turned to needles. We all gazed at the door.

A man was standing there. Water rolled off him like he were a monster risen from the sea. Behind him, the inn sign was yawing and screeching in the wind. The man peered at us from deep-set amber eyes that glowed in the shadows of his face like coals in the night. Then he bared his teeth in a devilish smile and entered without bothering to shut the door after him.

"I'm Captain Scratch," he announced in a deep, raspy voice.

Aunt Katy took his measure in an instant. "Why, I took you for the king of France, at least," she said. "Wipe your feet, sir.

Oliver, shut the door after the *gentleman,* and lay another plate."

Captain Scratch ripped open the buttons of his greatcoat and squeezed the rain out of his flaming beard as if he were wringing a chicken's neck. I stared at him. I'd seen that man before—through the spyglass. He was master of the *Sweet Molly.*

"Oliver," Aunt Katy whispered, giving me a prod of her elbow to uproot me from the floor. "Step lively."

Captain Scratch seated himself at a table along the wall, and without bothering to remove his beaver hat he ate two beefsteaks and three trenchers of chowder. He muttered a good deal to himself, ignoring the others in the room. That dark smile kept flashing across his face, and I heard Crick, the harpooner, mutter, "Captain Scratch, is he? From the look of him, mates, I'd as soon ship out with the Prince of Air himself!"—meaning the devil.

Little by little the room filled with laughter again, but it wasn't near as hearty as before. After he had finished eating, Captain Scratch wiped his lips with the end of his beard and called for a newspaper.

I fetched the first one I could find. He lit a long clay pipe and began reading. A moment later I saw that I had made a mistake—I had given him a newspaper that had been left behind by a China trader. It was printed in some peculiar language, but Captain Scratch was reading along as if it were the King's English.

By thunder, he doesn't know the difference, I realized. He can't read—he's just pretending. What kind of ship's master was he who didn't know his letters? A foc's'le hand could be as ignorant as a block of wood, but a captain had charts to study and the ship's log to write.

I was puzzling this over when Aunt Katy came out of the kitchen with a platter of fruit tarts—a birthday surprise. I was prodigiously fond of fruit tarts. She offered them to one and all, and a sailmaker slapped his leg and said it would suit him if I had a birthday twice a week.

"To tell the truth," Aunt Katy smiled. "Oliver has *two* birthdays at that. He was born at the stroke of midnight, was he— born straddling a Tuesday night and Wednesday morning. One day's as much his birthday as the other, although we came to favor the Wednesday of it."

At this Captain Scratch's nose lifted from the newspaper like a bowsprit rising from a sea swell. He clapped eyes on me as if, until that moment, he hadn't noticed my existence. For an instant his gaze lit up, and then he showed the white of his teeth in a twistical smile. "Avast there, boy!"

My heart took a leap into my throat.

"Come alongside, lad!"

"Yes, sir," I said.

"Born at the hour of midnight, were ye?"

"Aye, sir."

"At the very stroke?"

I said I'd been told as much.

"By the shrouds!" he said. "I've sailed the seven mongrel seas and only once before did I clap me eyes on one such as yourself. Born at the same dark hour, was old Billy Bombay! Aye, there's a wondrous power in it, I tell ye. A wondrous power, matey! It's Billy Bombay I'm combing the seas for. Have ye seen him, lad? Has he stopped in Nantucket waters, do ye know?"

"No, sir," I stammered. "At least, not here with us."

"Hackle his bones, he's leading me a merry chase! But he won't stay hid from his old shipmate, Harry Scratch." He began searching through his pockets. "Your birthday, is it, matey? Well, here's a Spanish doubloon for ye to remember Captain Scratch by."

The gold coin glittered between his fingers like a candle flame. "I couldn't accept it, sir," I answered. The truth was I didn't want anything to remember Captain Scratch by.

"Take it, boy!"

He pressed the doubloon in my hand, making a hard fist of it, and a moment later he was gone—leaving the door wide open to the shrieking wind.

I hung around the wharf most of the next afternoon. The *Sweet Molly* had tied up and was taking on fresh water and supplies. When the tide turned, two whalers put out to sea. The wind eased off and the sky hung overhead like milk glass. By late afternoon my father's ship had not made port.

"Of course not," Aunt Katy said when I got back to the Harpooner's Inn. "He's not a man to settle for a peaky, blustery, cheerless day like this for his homecoming. Mercy me, no. He likes to do a thing right, thy father, and when he comes sailing back it will be under a merry blue sky—a day befitting such a grand occasion. Now tomorrow, I'd say, tomorrow *might* do— with the weather breaking as it is."

Tomorrow then, I thought, and put my hopes on it.

Then she told me that Captain Scratch had sent word directing her to provide a pot of her famous cod chowder, for the ship's table.

"It's ready now," she added, swinging out the pothook. "After fetching it aboard, Oliver, stop in on Mr. Wicks. He was asking about thee again. He wants an apprentice without delay."

"Aunt Katy—I'd as soon be apprenticed to a Mohawk Indian."

"Along with thee, dearlove."

The next thing I knew I was hurrying along the wharves with a piping hot kettle of chowder between my hands. The *Sweet Molly* was tied up alongside and I was none too anxious to go aboard her. From the bulwarks her crew peered down at me like vultures. They were a ragged and fearsome-looking bunch, roasted brown by a southern sun. They numbered no more than fifteen or sixteen. Hardly a one of them was without a tooth missing or a cropped ear or a broken nose.

The first mate motioned me aboard. He was a tall scarecrow of a man with eyes like musket balls and a tarred pigtail that stood out from his head like a pan handle.

"Welcome to the *Bl*—I mean, to the *Sweet Molly*," he said, as if another name had all but slipped off the tip of his tongue. "Welcome to our humble ship, sonny. Don't spill a drop, now. The capting is waitin'."

It seemed to me that every man aboard was waiting for me. They were all a-grin. I made out a savage with Fiji hair and a hawk-faced man with a turban around his head. And then Captain Scratch himself appeared, rubbing his hands together over the rich odor of chowder—or so I fancied.

"Bring it along, me fine lad," he smiled. "This way, matey. Oliver, is it? There's a good, brave name—not afraid of the dark, are ye? I'll warrant you've seen your share of the dredgies, eh? This way, matey. Into the galley with it."

My only thought was to hand over the kettle and get my legs ashore. The passageway was dank as a cellar and I was discomfited by this talk of dredgies. Ghosts from the sea, they were—the spirits of drowned sailors.

"Step lively, boy."

Captain Scratch opened a door and I lugged the soup pot in with both hands. The galley was dark and silent. It had no galley smell at all. The next thing I knew Captain Scratch locked the door on me, and I heard his voice boom out:

"Cast off, shipmates! The tide's on the turn. Put to sea, me fine jailbirds!"

CHAPTER 2

In which I am at sea,
in more ways than one

I WAS a prisoner in that foul room for two days. I spent the first day trying to kick the door down, and the second nursing my foot. It took a monstrous lot of the fight out of me, which is no doubt what Captain Scratch had in mind.

I dreamed of seeing him hung in chains and his crew of grinning wasters as well. What did they want with me? At this very moment my father might well have reached Nantucket. After waiting three endless years—I'd missed him!

My fury rose and fell like a fever. If I had yearned for a ship under my feet, I had not bargained for the *Sweet Molly.* Plaguey ship! The best of it was that I had no doubt surprised old Mr. Wicks, the barrelmaker, by disappearing from the face of the earth.

Meanwhile, the ship creaked and groaned through the seas.

From the piles of moldering canvas at my fingertips I knew that I was bolted up in the sail locker. I slept on canvas, and whenever I felt hungry I dipped into the chowder kettle—cold, but nourishing.

Of course my father would come looking for me. He might get the whole Nantucket fleet to set sail. Jack Crick might board us at any moment with his harpoon and run Captain Scratch clear through—and dance an Irish clog on his beard.

I was sound asleep on a mound of canvas when I awoke to find the door wide open and the first mate standing over me. He poked me with a bony finger as long as a stick.

"Strike me ugly!" he said in a cackling voice. "Why, if it ain't that nice lad from Nantucket. Mornin' to ye, sonny. Forgot to go ashore when we cast off, did ye?"

I sat up sharply. If I knew a thing about dogs it was never to let on that you were afraid, and to a man these were curs and hounds of the sea. They were not going to get the bettermost of me. I looked him in the eye. "Forgot?" said I. "No such thing, sir! I was locked in—as you know well enough!"

"Locked in, say ye?" He clucked his tongue and rolled his musket-ball eyes in mock astonishment. "That door *does* have a nasty way of warpin' itself shut. Now, sonny, what brand of seaworm would lock ye in, I ask?"

"Captain Scratch himself," I answered.

His shark's teeth shone in the gloom. "A fine gent like that? Why, I give ye the word of John Ringrose there's no kinder soul on the high seas than our good Capting Scratch. Why, his heart's as true as a church bell, it is—and just as large."

"Stuff!" said I, surprised by my own bluster.

He screwed down one eye. "Aye, but the capting don't like a

stowaway aboard his ship, not him. I do hope he won't get down his cat-o'-nine-tails when he sets his lamps on ye, sonny."

"Stowaway!" I sputtered.

"Aye."

"Why—I'm not the least bit of a stowaway, sir!"

He shifted his weight and gave me a chuckle. "Oh, ye can count on John Ringrose to put in a good word for ye. Here, now, let's tidy ye up a bit, sonny—we want ye to look yer best for the capting." He dusted off my wool coat and raked back my tangled hair with his fingers. "That's the ticket. Why, yuv got an honest face, lad, and that's in yer favor. And seaman's eyes—I spied that right off. Blue, ain't they? Blue as the Indian Ocean itself. Topside with ye, sonny."

I was glad enough to see daylight even though a cold mist hung over the sea. The sun was burning through like an evil eye and I saw at once that we were on a southerly course.

"Capting!" John Ringrose shouted, taking me by the collar and walking me up the ladder to the poop deck. "See here what I flushed out of the foc'sle for ye."

Captain Scratch stood squinting at the weather. When he saw me his eyebrows shot aloft. "The devil fetch me," he exclaimed, innocent as a lamb. "Why, it's young Oliver Finch."

His legs were thrust into deep boots and he had a bull's hide thrown across his shoulders against the raw weather. The very sight of this man stopped my breath short. He towered over me like a great hairy beast and I wanted to streak it. But I was resolved not to betray my faint-heartedness. My father would plant his legs firmly on deck and give this villain a calm but lofty glance, and I tried to do the same.

"Run off to sea, have ye, lad?"

"Not a bit, sir," said I.

"Found him hid away in the sail locker," John Ringrose clucked.

"A stowaway! Lord save me, that means the cat-o'-nine-tails."

"I do hope ye won't be too hard on him, Capting," Mr. Ringrose sighed. "Why, there's hardly as much flesh on his ribs as a pullet. I'd rather take a lashing on me own hide than see the cat laid to a lad of his tender years."

I stiffened my back. "You can't scarify me, sir," I declared. That was so far from the truth it was a monstrous lie. My heart was banging away like thunder.

"There *is* extenuatin' circumstances," the first mate went on. "Bein' that the door jammed shut of its own will, as the boy says."

"I said no such thing," I protested. They ignored me and parleyed over my head. You'd think *I* was the villain instead of Captain Scratch.

John Ringrose licked his lips. "Now, bein' a *merciful* man, Capting, known from Tortuga to Zanzibar for yer tender ways, Capting—why, I wouldn't put it past ye to let the boy off on good behavior."

Between the two of them there was more mercy to be found in a keg of fishhooks, I thought.

"Well spoke, Mr. Ringrose," Captain Scratch declared, full of thought, as if he were a lord of the Admiralty deciding a case of law. "Aye, I'll belay the cat, the boy meaning no harm."

"Bless ye, Capting," the first mate nodded, giving me a wink as if to prod me into thanking Captain Scratch for his leniency.

"I'll thank you, sir," said I, "first to tell me why you carried me off to sea, and second, sir, to put me ashore as soon as possible!"

"Touchy as gunpowder, ain't he?" Mr. Ringrose laughed.

"Aye, temperish like Billy Bombay himself!" the captain said. His eyes glowed up like balls of St. Elmo's fire. "Always one to speak his mind, was old Billy. Well, now I think of it, ye might be special useful on this voyage, Oliver Finch. Special useful."

"Mark my word, sir," I answered, wishing I could stop sounding so peskily polite. "When my father gets wind of your mischief he'll fetch you alongside like a whale and boil you down for the oil in your hide, sir!"

"Did ye hear that, Mr. Ringrose!" the captain roared. "Scraped down for lamp fuel!"

"The Lord save us," the first mate croaked.

"Why, boy, it pains me to hear ye hold such an unfriendly opinion of me," Captain Scratch said. "I wouldn't hold ye aboard ship against your will for all the sugar in Jamaica. Hackle me bones, if I would! If it's land ye want under your feet, land it'll be. Aye, trust Harry Scratch to put ye ashore, lad. At the very first opportunity. Why, matey, you're as free as a seabird!"

At that moment there came a high shout from the lookout at the masthead. "Ship ahoy!"

The smile dropped like a mask from Captain Scratch's face.

The bows of a whaler cut through the sea mist on the starboard side. My heart took a leap. I thought it was my father's ship come to rescue me. But then, as I made out the carved figurehead under the bowsprit, I recognized the *Jonas' Revenge*. She was the fastest ship in the Nantucket fleet.

Instantly John Ringrose clapped a hand over my mouth and pulled me down out of sight behind the bulwark—and Captain Scratch rested a foot on my neck. Free as a seabird, was I!

"Avast, there!" came a shout from the whaler. "Do you have Oliver Finch aboard?"

"Who do ye say?" answered Captain Scratch in a pious voice, as if he'd never heard the name before.

"Captain Isaiah Finch's boy!"

"Run away to sea, has he?"

"Not likely, sir! Not with his father due home any day."

"We carry no passengers aboard the *Sweet Molly*," shouted the captain.

I began to struggle, but Mr. Ringrose tightened up on my mouth and Captain Scratch leaned more heavily with his foot. I found myself squinting along the deck planks—and thought for an instant I was seeing things.

There was Jibboom!

He was curled up on a tackle block looking at me. He had followed me aboard, tracking me in his usual way. For the first time I could remember, I was glad to see that cat. But even as I struggled he merely peered at me with his one eye and made no move at all to help me.

The palaver was still flying between the two ships. If my father had not yet made port, I fancied it was Aunt Katy who had roused the whaling men to search for me. "The boy was seen going aboard the *Sweet Molly*, sir!" I recognized the voice of my friend Jack Crick, the harpooner.

"We were not the only ship to sail with the tide," answered Captain Scratch. "The lad stowed away in one of those blubber-boilers of yours, as likely as not." Then he dropped the bull's hide off his shoulders and gave John Ringrose a quick sign to get me below decks. "But you're welcome aboard, gentlemen, if it'll please ye!"

"We'll lower a boat!"

The first mate lost no time. He tied his kerchief around my mouth, rolled me in the mangy hide, bent me over his shoulder like a carpet, and carried me down the hatch. But Jack Crick wouldn't be fooled, I thought. He'd know I was aboard. He'd know the moment he saw Jibboom and recognized him for Aunt Katy's one-eyed cat!

Deeper into the ship we went. My heart was already in my throat, but when I saw Jibboom following me—I very nearly choked. Lower and lower we went with Jibboom keeping a few paces behind. I tried to shout to him through the kerchief in my mouth, but he kept coming—tracking me like a catamount.

Finally we were down at the very bottom of the ship, down among the ballast stone, and there we stayed—Mr. Ringrose, Jibboom and I.

"Not so much as a breath out of ye, boy," warned the first mate, "or I'll be obliged to wring yer neck like a chicken."

He kept the kerchief tightly tied through my mouth. We sat huddled in the bull's hide against the cold and dampness of the stones. I gazed upward through the dark and thought of Jack Crick and the others poking about the decks. They were so near! But they'd never find me in this black hole.

I was by turns heavy-hearted and so enormous mad that I tried to chew the kerchief in two. I wished my father were here. He'd take one look about and begin knocking heads together.

By thunder! So would I. The idea jerked me to my senses. There wasn't a moment to lose. Opportunity lay piled all about me, and John Ringrose had not thought to bind up my hands. I would take hold of a ballast stone and lay him out!

I was careful not to alert him. I dropped my hands and felt about my legs, slowly, inch by inch. He attempted to amuse me and pass the time by telling me of his adventures. He had run off to sea, been twice shipwrecked, captured by Spaniards and once marooned—before his fifteenth birthday. "Aye, I know what it is to be terrible afraid and alone in the world, lad—like yerself."

By this time I had taken a firm purchase on a ballast stone. I was in a prickly sweat that Jack Crick and the others might leave before I could streak it topside. I set my muscles, took a breath—but couldn't raise the stone an inch! It was so enormous heavy it felt bolted down.

My fingers quickly took the measure of something smaller.

"Aye, sonny, yuv got a friend in John Ringrose. I'll not let any harm come to ye aboard this ship."

I found a rock the size of a cannonball. I hesitated. I was surprised to find that I would be sorry to clap him on the head with it. But I would be sorrier still to be left aboard this infernal ship, and did what I had to do.

The blow caught him square on the top of the head. I was ready to run for it. But all the stone did was jar a laugh out of him. "Strike me ugly!" he said, catching my ankle. "That was a credit to ye. Aye, if I didn't have a skull like an anvil, sonny, ye'd have filled it with birdsong. Why, with high spirits like that ye'll rise to be an admiral, at least. Now rest easy, and I'll tell ye how I escaped from the Spaniards. Before this voyage is finished I'll learn ye yer ropes and riggin's and ye'll thank me for it."

I sunk into the blackest despair. In time a shout came ringing down the hold. The Nantucket men had returned to their ship. Mr. Ringrose untied the kerchief from my mouth, but it was too late to call out. I could see Jibboom's lone eye gazing out of the blackness. Plaguey cat! We were set adrift now, the two of us, aboard the foul *Sweet Molly.*

"Where, sir, are we bound for?" I asked hopelessly.

"Well now, mate, leave it to the capting to set us a fine course."

"But what does he want with me?"

"Born at the stroke of midnight, weren't ye? Like Billy Bombay? When he's ready the capting will give ye a pretty answer!"

He'd say no more, and we made our way across the wet ballast stones. Feeling ahead of me, I stumbled into cannons and balls.

"Aye, cannons they are," Mr. Ringrose laughed. "And enough iron balls and grapeshot to settle any argument that comes looking for us, shipmate."

As we climbed out of the hold I gazed back down the ladder and wondered what strange manner of ship was the *Sweet Molly*.

CHAPTER 3

Of dredgies, and how I planned to outfox Captain Scratch with a plank of wood

THE *SWEET Molly* went skulking through the seas and kept beyond the sight of land.

The thought of escape or rescue was never far from my mind. The captain decided that the only work I was fitted for was grommet, or ship's boy. "Aye, and ye can start by fetching me a flagon of wine and a biscuit."

I had got over my fear of him somewhat, at least when a good temper was on him, but I saw no reason to serve him. "I'm obliged to remind you, sir," said I, "that I have not signed the ship's articles and am therefore not a member of your crew." My father could not have said it better, I told myself, and took courage from that.

He was bareheaded to the wind and his beard was whipping

about as gaily as a pennant. "The devil fetch me—didn't I tell ye, lad? I signed on *for* ye."

He walked me to the mainmast and deeply carved was the roster of the crew. All had signed themselves with an X except one, who had cut in all the letters of the name he sailed under— Jack o' Lantern. I knew him as the second mate.

"That's our ship's articles!" Captain Scratch laughed, giving the mast a tap. "And this X mark here—it's yourself, boy. Can't ye read your own name?"

"Yes, sir," I said, knowing he had got the best of me. "But not spelled that way."

"It'll do. Fetch me that wine!"

Grommet, was I? I was determined to be the worst grommet ever born. I found a barrel of moldy sea biscuits in the pantry and chose the wormiest one of the lot. When I returned on deck, Captain Scratch was having the bottom sails wet for speed, as they held the wind better that way. He half-emptied the wine flagon in a gulp. The biscuit was hard as mortar, but he didn't seem to notice. He bit off a piece and spit out the worms like grape seeds, and sent me back for more. There was no getting the best of that man.

I slept in a narrow wooden bunk in the crew's quarters, for-ward, in the foc'sle. Seawater oozed from every seam and dripped from the timbers. Light and air hardly reached down there, and day and night tobacco smoke hung about the com-partment like a damp sea fog.

And there were peculiar goings-on aboard that ship. For one thing, Captain Scratch kept a lamp burning in his cabin all night long. He was afraid to sleep in the dark. He was, in fact, forever cursing the dredgies. He had a mortal fear they might board the ship at night and slit his throat. Mr. Ringrose told me that himself. Throughout the dark hours a sailor made the rounds, swinging a lantern along the weather decks to frighten off any boarding spirits. They could no more be seen than the wind, but the briny ghosts left wet footprints, and that gave them away for sure. The man on dredgy watch kept his eyes peeled for the drip of footprints.

I was not long in finding a way to get myself rescued. It was the carvings on the mainmast that put the idea in my head. All I needed was a jackknife, and I had that. I would carve a message in one of my bunk slats and set it adrift.

I had to wait until the crew was snoring and the whale-oil lamp was turned low. Then I'd pull aside the edge of the mattress and carve away. I took my time and cut the message deep. If anyone stirred, I stopped. If a foc'sle hand walked in, I pretended to be asleep. Jibboom found a beam to suit him and would spend the night hours gazing at me with that wise old eye of his. I had got over being angry at him and, in fact, he was a comfort to me—although we still weren't speaking overly much.

I was two nights working on that message, but finally I cut in the last of it. It read:

HELP. AM PRISONER ABOARD SWEET MOLLY. ON SOUTHERLY COURSE FROM NANTUCKET.

OLIVER FINCH, AGE 12

The next day I waited until the foc'sle was deserted and set to work digging out the nails to free the board. I was hard at it when I saw Jibboom's back shoot up. I turned. Captain Scratch was standing behind me with a hard squint in his eye.

"What's this, boy?" he scowled.

Thunder and lightning! I was found out. I was doomed. Then it came to me that Captain Scratch didn't know his letters. He couldn't read—he only pretended. I looked him in the eye and decided to brazen it out.

"As you see for yourself, sir," I said. "I've carved my family motto—for luck, sir."

"For luck, do ye say?"

"Yes, sir."

He scratched through his fiery beard, glaring at me, and then pushed me aside. He screwed up one eye and peered at the message.

"Blast me eyeballs, mate, this ain't much light to read by."

"No, sir."

"Me lamps ain't as strong seeing as when I was your age. Family motto, is it?"

"Yes, sir."

"Aye, I'm beginning to make it out."

"I may have misspelled a word or two," I said, while my mind raced ahead trying to think up something that would pass for a motto.

He tried the other eye. "Ye write a good hand, I can see that."

"With the words spelled wrong it makes hard reading, no doubt," I added, sure of myself now.

"Aye, it's the misspellings that's throwing me."

"It means to say—" I had the motto now. "I mean, what it says is, *Let the heart of a Finch never fail.*"

"So it does!" he nodded, a smile shooting out of his face. "I can see it clear now, I can. But never did I come across *heart* spelled in that peculiar way. That's where ye went wrong, matey. Well, now, that's a fine motto to sleep on."

He turned and was gone.

But no passing ship, I told myself, was going to stop for a floating plank of wood. My message might drift through the seas for months—years, even.

Why hadn't I thought of that before? What a blockhead I was! It was a marvel that I could see an inch beyond my nose. I had just the thing—the gold doubloon Captain Scratch himself had pressed on me.

I dug the coin out of my pocket. I shined it up bright as a mirror. Finding a moment to be alone I nailed it to the center of my message. That was bound to catch some lookout's eye, flashing in the sun—providing the slat landed right side up in the water.

I'd see to that.

I let myself into the sail locker and cut off a hundred feet of stout twine. Now I was ready, and there was even a cold white slice of moon rising in the sky to help me.

I waited until the dredgy watch had gone by and there was only the wash and hiss of the sea along the bows. I hung back in the deepest shadows of the quarterdeck, my senses alert. I could see Jack o' Lantern, the second mate, at the ship's wheel high above on the poop deck. He was the very image of his name, a large fat man with a prodigious appetite. A wide belt girded his stomach like a barrel hoop. He was singing away merrily to himself and the stars.

Silently, I let the plank over the side by the sailmaker's twine. If it landed wrong side up I'd haul it back and try again. But luck was with me. In a flash I saw the doubloon catch the moonlight, and let the string go. My heart took a leap—the message was on its way. I watched until the winking doubloon had disappeared along the wake. I was bound to be rescued now and silently thanked Captain Scratch for the use of his Spanish coin.

But now it came to me that Jack o' Lantern's singing voice was no longer in the air. I looked up—and there he was peering down. His round face had a huge grin on it.

I turned to stone. He was certain to bring the ship about and fish out the plank and discover my mischief. We stood gazing into each other's eyes and not a word passed between us. Finally I heard a laugh under his breath and gathered hope from it. "Can ye steer a ship, bucko?" he asked.

"Yes, sir." That wasn't strictly the truth.

"For sure and certain?"

"I'm not certain I *can't* steer a ship," I said.

He called me up to the wheel and told me the course and let me try to hold it. For a while that ship lurched about like a scrap of paper in the wind, but I did finally get something of the hang of it.

As for the plank of wood, Jack o' Lantern asked me no questions and in the days ahead he kept his own counsel.

CHAPTER 4

*Being full of knives and
pistols and omens of my future*

DAYS GATHERED, weeks passed, but not a sign did I see
of another ship. Captain Scratch had laid his cruise
wide of the sea lanes. But still I did not despair. One morning a
lone bird came fluttering down on our yardarm. After resting
there most of the day, he flew off again. I sorely envied him his
wings.

Except for Mr. Ringrose, who busied me with ropes and
knots, and Jack o' Lantern, who exercised my mind with the
stars overhead, I never saw such a lazy crew of wasters. They
did no more work than it took to sail the ship and caulk the
leaks and stand the watches. Not once did I see a man draw up
a bucket of water to wash his clothes—for they never took them
off. Not once did I see the decks swabbed down. My father

would have tossed this pack of beggars overboard, but Captain Scratch seemed hugely pleased with them.

The sea air was turning balmy, and no longer did he appear on deck in his bull's hide. We were entering the southern latitudes. Every afternoon he'd send me for a tongue of salt beef, of which he was enormous fond, and pace between the rails, whittling and eating off the blade of his knife.

The nights were now a blaze of stars. The *Sweet Molly* seemed at ease in these waters, like a homing pigeon returned, and one night I asked Jack o' Lantern where we might be by the map.

"Sniff that air?" he answered, giving me a large smile. He was at the helm again and his round, pumpkin face glowed in the binnacle lamp. "That's Spanish wind in our sails, me fine young gentleman, and if ye don't want yer throat cut ye'll keep yer eyes skinned for sea rovers and suchlike. We're approaching the old Spanish Main, shipmate—aye, and there'll be blood for breakfast if we're caught napping."

He ripped out a bull-throated laugh and I fancied that he was only trying to amuse me by stretching things a bit. But several times during the night I awoke to the clank of chains and heavy scraping sounds along the passageways. In the dark hours of morning I heard John Ringrose's crackling laughter rise from the hold and Jibboom leaped to my bunk. We peered at each other for a moment, eye to eye, and then he walked down my leg and curled himself at my feet. I let him stay.

In the morning we awoke to find ourselves aboard a different ship with a different crew. Gold rings dangled from almost every ear. Belts bristled with pistols and knives. Cannons had been hauled up from the hold and lashed in position along the decks. Swivel guns were dropped in place at the bulwarks. We were armed to the teeth like a man-o'-war.

And in the midst of it all stood Captain Scratch shouting oaths and orders in a voice to make the sea rumble. His head was tied up in a blood-red scarf, and his eyes danced with a kind of sinister delight. Three knives and three pistols were jammed into his silken waistband. A cutlass flashed in his hand with every command.

"Blast ye, Hajji!" he roared, slicing the air toward a Red Sea sailor with a turban wound round his head. "Get aloft, ye hawk-eyed gallows bird. Ezra Fly! Big Nose Ned! The sternboard, mates, the sternboard! Cannibal! Where is that flesh-eating bo'sun? Haul up our colors, ye Fiji-headed savage! Finch! Lend a hand or I'll slice ye in two!"

It was a moment before I realized his cutlass was flashing at me, and then I stepped lively.

"Lookout! If ye see so much as a pocket handkerchief on the horizon, sing out! If ye miss anything I'll serve ye up to the bo'sun for dinner!"

The ship was being refurbished, fore and aft, before my eyes. I found myself at the stern and gave a hand. Ezra Fly, the ship's carpenter, went over the side on a rope and soon we were hauling in a heavy nameplate that had been fixed across the sternboard. It bore the name *Sweet Molly* like a mask.

I bent over the rail to see what name the false plate had concealed. Suddenly, I recollected the day I had come aboard when Mr. Ringrose had welcomed me to the "*Bl*—I mean," he had said, "the *Sweet Molly*." Now I began to make out the upside-down letters across the stern—the true name of the ship.

The *Bloody Hand*!

The name sent a cold shiver through me. That was no fit name for a ship—or anything else. My hopes for rescue faded on the instant. I would not be found. Any ship coming upon my message would expect to find me aboard the *Sweet Molly,* but the *Sweet Molly* was no more. It was all for nothing.

I turned as a shout went up. Cannibal, his Fiji hair standing about his head like a great thistle bloom, was running up a different flag. When it snapped open with the wind I was struck dumb. It was the flag of the Wicked Order of Sea Robbers. It was the skull and crossbones!

"Welcome to the *Bloody Hand!*" John Ringrose cackled beside me. "Yer on the account now, sonny—a-roving with as fine a bunch of pirate cutthroats as ever sailed on one ship!"

Unmasked now, the ship went swaggering before the wind as if with a knife clamped between her teeth. Captain Scratch had a cask of rum lashed to the mainmast and punctured it like a sieve with the tip of his cutlass. The crew swarmed around like flies, their red mouths flung open to the streams of grog.

By nightfall, half the buccaneers were in their cups, singing and brawling, and the other half lay as limp as canvas here and there about the decks.

I had heard bloody tales in Nantucket, stories of the old Brethren of the Coast, as they called their outcast society—of Morgan and Blackbeard, Tew and Captain Kidd. To go on the account was to go murdering and plundering on the high seas. If Captain Scratch thought to make a brigand of me, he had the wrong pig by the tail.

With this firm resolution simmering in my blood, I knocked at the door of his cabin.

"Aye!" he shouted. The door was ajar and now it swung open with the slow roll of the ship. Captain Scratch sat with his coat flung open and one jackbooted leg thrust up on his chart table. A pewter mug hung empty in his hand and at his elbow stood the cutlass with its point sunk in the deck.

"Captain," I said stoutly. "Sir—"

"Come in, matey," he interrupted, his face aglow with rum. Overhead a lamp swung slowly in its shining brass gimbals, sending shadows traveling back and forth along the walls. "Bless the mark, I was about to pipe ye to me cabin. Sit ye down."

"I can say what needs saying on my feet," I replied.

"Avast, grommet!" he roared. "Sit ye down! What I have to say will tire your calf's legs."

He lifted the cutlass, struck a nearby chair and hurled it at me. The man filled me with dread. The smiles that flared and shifted across his mouth did nothing to improve the wild disorder of his face. I caught the chair in midair. I sat myself down, keeping an eye on the door for sudden escape.

"A complaint have ye, shipmate?"

"I have, sir," I said.

"Has one of me water rats touched a hair of your head, eh? Name him, boy, and I'll heave him to the sharks!"

I shook my head. "I have no complaint there. The truth is, I am treated civil enough."

"Aye," he chuckled. "Those are me orders. Why, good pious lads, they are—every one a parson's son. Then what agitates ye, boy?"

I tried to look him square in the eye, which was no easy task. "It's one thing to be impressed aboard this ship, but it's something else, sir, to be put on the account. In short, I don't intend to join you and your sea robbers at Execution Dock."

Laughter burst from his throat. "Execution Dock, say ye! Aye, we'd make a merry harvest for the hangman. But ye have me word for it, mate, we'll not be dancing to the hemp. Take the word of Harry Scratch, and rest easy."

I had already known him to give his word in one breath and break it in the next. His promise wasn't worth a copper.

"Now, belay that gallows talk," he grinned, with a yellow flash of teeth. His voice lowered to a heavy whisper. "Come closer, Oliver Finch, and I'll tell ye what the future holds for ye. Aye, your fortune, boy, such as no gypsy ever told ye. Listen, you'll wear plumes in your hat and a coat of velvet on your back—with gold a-jangling in your pockets as heavy as nails. And jewels, lad—rubies and emeralds in your sea chest as thick as grapes on the vine." His eyes were feverishly lit with greed. "Riches, boy, treasures such as never crossed your mind—a king's ransom up for shares. The devil seize me soul if I'm stretching the truth! Varlets will bow and scrape as ye walk along the street. Aye, a gentleman is reckoned by the weight of his gold, and gentlemen we'll be by the ton! No, matey, I'll not fetch ye to Gallows' Point—we'll lay a different course. We'll ride through the streets of London Town in coaches as gold as the sun and the envy of every lord and judge of the realm. Mark what I say!"

I held my ground. "I don't want your hat plumes and chests of gold," I said, for I hardly believed a word of what he said. "And as for apprenticing myself to cutthroats and murderers, I don't fancy that trade."

"Cutthroats! Hackle me bones, ye do have a sharp tongue for your years. Ye do me and me honest seamen an injustice. Why, there ain't one of us that ever cut a man's throat—except he was deserving of it. The bo'sun, I'll grant ye, takes a relish in it, being a flesheater—born and raised in the cannibal isles. But he's partial to Spaniards only—so you've nothing to fear of him."

"Sir," I said. "You will do me a service by putting me ashore."

"Ashore, say ye? Where, may I ask, would suit ye?"

"I won't be at all particular."

"Along the Mosquito Coast, then? A fine place for ye that would be. Why, in ten minutes those Honduras savages would have ye so full of arrows you'd look like a porcupine. Maybe you'd rather be set down on the shores of Hispaniola for the Spaniards to put in chains? Well, what's your choice, boy!"

I was silent.

"Do ye think," he scowled, "I plucked ye off the Nantucket dock without your best interests in me heart? Would ye now desert us, matey, when I've spread before ye riches as would make the Grand Mogul's mouth water?"

"If you give me a choice," I said, "I would be put aboard some passing ship."

"By the shrouds, was there ever such an ungrateful whelp!" He rose in a haze of rum fumes and I thought for an instant he would lunge at me with the cutlass. But then, like a shifting wind, he began to chuckle and fell back in his chair with the name of Billy Bombay on his lips. At every turn I seemed to put him in mind of his old shipmate. "A banty cock of a man, was Billy—no bigger than a flyboat, and him full grown. But quick as a shark and twice as deadly, lad. Aye, and I'd still be trying to clap deadlights on him but for me young friend, Oliver Finch. The devil fetch Billy Bombay now that I have ye to guide me—ye that was born at the same midnight hour."

What my having been born at that hour had to do with pirate treasure seemed beyond reckoning.

Suddenly he swept a chart to the floor and held it open with his boots spread apart. He peered at the map as if he could read the markings, and when he looked up his voice was a whisper again. "Treasure, did I say? Aye, treasure enough to swamp a ship, and you're in for a share, lad." He leaned toward me, so close now that I could see the veins in his nose, like a tangle of red threads.

"Hear me, mate, this is no pirate's tale such as is bandied about the drink houses of Tortuga or Spanish Town. With me own eyes have I seen this golden feast. With me own hands have I buried it. Aye, misburied in me mind, ye might say, but you'll be me pilot fish and lead me to it."

He kept bending closer, inch by inch, until it seemed our noses were touching. "Seven years it's been, matey! Seven years mouldering in the black sands of Gentleman Jack's island! Don't bother spying at me charts, shipmate—ye won't find it. But I know where it hides, that island, and before the week is out you'll be setting foot ashore."

"Gentleman Jack?" I asked.

"Aye. He was master of this very ship, boy—and me his second mate in those days. He filled our hold with plunder snatched from Hispaniola itself. Aye, a great commander was Gentleman Jack—not a man of the brethren wouldn't give up his right arm to serve before the sticks with him. A true gent he was, too, as could write his name with the flourish of the governor of Jamaica. He could quote the Greeks to ye out of one side of his mouth and shout an oath out of the other to melt the tar off your pigtail."

"Is he dead?"

"Aye, these seven years dead—murdered before me eyes by fiendish treachery, boy. There were six of us ashore to bury the loot—there being so much burden to it. He led us so many twists and turns to the spot as would make the head of a dervish spin. And at night, too, with no more light from the moon than a binnacle lamp. But he had cat's eyes, did Gentleman Jack, and took his bearings as if it were day. Marked them as we went on the white of his shirtsleeve. Aye, dipped the nib of his quill in a lump of fruit he had plucked on the Hispaniola shore—writing with the black juice like it was ink."

He paused to unburden himself of a string of oaths, and went on.

"We were a merry lot, with a bit of rum in us, and finally, deep in the island, he stopped—and there we dug the pit. And there we lowered the chests. Then a shot took us by surprisal and across the pit I saw Gentleman Jack heave out a gasp. He tumbled into the pit, dead before he fell across those chests of plunder. Beside me stood the chief mate with smoke rising from his pistol like a wisp of moonlight. 'Avast, brethren,' says he. 'I'm captain now!' And so he was for the space of ten seconds. I throttled him on the spot—such was me loyalty to Gentleman Jack, may his timbers rest in peace."

Captain Scratch slowly leaned back, so the distance between our noses increased. "I cut off his white shirtsleeve meself, with the bearings marked, and we covered him and the treasure over with sand. The chief mate we left to the wild boars to feast on. The rest of us returned to the *Bloody Hand*. I was elected captain and we returned to the sea lanes in the natural pursuit of our calling."

Captain Scratch fell silent, sunk in his own dark thoughts. Despite myself, his tale stirred my imagination. Finally I said, "Do you not still have the shirtsleeve?"

He awoke from his grim reverie and fixed his eyes on me. "Ye want a look at it, do ye?" He lifted a white rag from the chart table with the point of his blade and dangled it before my eyes as if to tempt me with it. And then, to my surprise, he dropped the shirtsleeve into my lap.

It was age-yellowed, frayed at one end, and with a blood-stained lace cuff at the other. I stretched it between my hands to locate the bearings, and then looked up in some bafflement. "There's nothing marked on this sleeve."

"Aye!" he rumbled. "That's the truth of it—not a mark, eh? He smelled treachery, did Gentleman Jack, and would have the final laugh if any of us thought to plunder the treasure for himself. We locked his sleeve in an iron chest, and there it stayed until the *Bloody Hand* returned to the island. When we opened the chest, the markings had faded from sight. He knew his inks, did Gentleman Jack, and his crew even better. Not one of us left alive had the exact bearings fixed in his mind. We scurried about like sand crabs trying to locate the old twists and turns. We've returned to the island time and again, we have, and dug the place into a thousand anthills. But Gentleman Jack's treasure grave has give us the slip."

Then, suddenly, Captain Scratch was swaying on his feet, grinning as if he'd have the best of the bargain. "But we'll not fail again, matey! Twice ashore did I get a whiff of brimstone on the breeze. Do ye not know what that means?"

"Brimstone, sir?"

"Aye, the smell of ghosts, lad! Sulphur enough to choke your nostrils. Gentleman Jack rests uneasy in his grave. He struts the island, I tell ye, as sure as the old queen's ghost walks the Tower of London. A vaporous gentleman is he, aye, with the scent of hell itself clinging to him. Mark me, at this very instant he frets and paces that murderous grave like it was his own quarter-deck!"

I was not one to scoff at shades and spirits, being of an open mind in these dark matters. But thunder and lightning!—this old cutthroat was sorely possessed by dredgies and ghosts. "Have you seen the spirit?" I asked.

He replied with a glowering look as if I hadn't any sense at all. "*Seen* him? Why, if I could clap deadlights on him that treasure would have been in the hold before this. I'd watch him sink into his grave and spy the very ground to dig. *Seen* him? Haven't ye been told, boy? Don't ye know that the power to *see* the sulphurous gentry falls only to swabs like Billy Bombay and yourself—aye, babes born at midnight have the ghostly gift, and none other! That's why I've raked the seas for old Billy—that's why I hauled ye aboard. You'll be me eyes, boy! Together, we'll watch for Gentleman Jack, and you'll show us where to sink our spades!"

CHAPTER 5

Containing events too horrible to mention

I WAS hugely surprised to know that I had the power to see ghosts. Later, in my bunk, with Jibboom curled at my feet, I turned this midnight matter over in my head.

If I had such powers why had no ghosts passed before my eyes during all my twelve years? Aunt Katy, I now recalled, had once been troubled by a prankster spirit—a boggart, as she called it—who in the dead of winter kept pulling the quilt off the foot of her bed so that she caught cold. While she hadn't *seen* the boggart, she *did* have the head cold to prove it.

And then it came to me that if I had not yet laid eyes on a ghost, it was because they shied about in the very dark of night. They were to be seen only during those hours when I slept. And as I was a sound sleeper I had never caught the merest glimpse of the night creatures.

While I was glad to learn of my ghosting powers, I was dubersome about it, too. I was seized by the desire to put the matter to the test. To go adventuring after a ghost was more to my fancy than sea-robbing and throat-cutting. It put a different light on things. The chance would present itself soon enough when we fetched up at Gentleman Jack's island.

But other thoughts went flashing through my mind. Certain details in Captain Scratch's account troubled me. Of the ghosts of murdered men I knew this, that they could not rest in their graves until justice had been done them. They walked abroad during the black hours seeking revenge.

Why, then, did Gentleman Jack lie uneasy in his grave? He had been avenged on the spot. Captain Scratch himself had squared the account by throttling the chief mate and leaving him for the wild boars.

I was somewhere along in these thoughts when I fell asleep. I was awakened hours later by a great shudder that cracked overhead like thunder. At the same time the ship gave a lurch that pitched three men out of their bunks. In the sleepy confusion that followed, during which no one was sure what had happened, shouts echoed along the dim passageway and the bo'sun's pipe sang out.

The rum-sodden buccaneers went staggering topside, myself among them. Captain Scratch was already on deck, shouting orders and cursing to the skies.

"Aloft! Get aloft, ye lazy swine! Mariners of the devil! Dance me a jig on those footropes!"

A howling windstorm had dropped out of the sky and struck us with the suddenness of lightning. The mainsail had cracked open like an overripe melon. The ends went leaping and twisting in the wind. The rotting canvas had split with a thunderous clap, bringing every man awake, and now Cannibal led several hands up the ratlines.

"Strip that canvas, ye bilge-water rats!" the captain shouted. "Aye, the storms is tricksy in these latitudes, mates. Mr. Ringrose! Jack o' Lantern! Rig us up some fresh laundry!"

I could do seaman's work. I had, in fact, started toward the riggings when Captain Scratch caught me by the leg. His fingers dug into my flesh like a grappling hook. "Where in damnation do ye think you're going, grommet!" he asked in a rough whisper.

"Aloft."

"You'll stay out of harm's way, boy, or I'll flog the hide off ye!"

He pulled me off the ratlines and threw me aside. It was clear enough what he was thinking. If anything happened to me the voyage would come to nothing. My work was on the island.

I sat on one of the bronze deck cannons to watch, and Jibboom appeared out of nowhere to sharpen his claws on the water barrel. The spare mainsail was brought up from the locker, bent to its boom on deck, and hauled aloft on a gantline. The sail was sheeted home, and the canvas bellied out with the wind. The howler had passed almost as suddenly as it had arrived. It was not yet daybreak.

I could make out the shapes of men still aloft, gliding back along the footropes toward the safety of the mainmast. They seemed to be walking on the air itself.

Then, with a sudden roll of the ship, the footrope parted and snapped free like a whip.

The men came hurling through the air. Their blood-chilling screams followed them down like comet tails. They went plunging into the black sea. For the instant I was too horrified even to gasp.

A dread stillness followed, hardly a sound, except for the slow crash of the sea and the idle flapping of the broken rope against the canvas. I rushed to the rail and skinned my eyes for some splash of arms below.

"By the shrouds!" came the voice of Captain Scratch. "I'll warrant not a one of them can swim a stroke. Helmsman!"

As he gave the order to bring the ship around, I looked up and saw a lone figure climb down out of the shadows of the riggings. It was Cannibal, who had already reached the mast when the footrope parted.

"How many?" Jack o' Lantern asked.

"T'ree," answered the Fiji bo'sun.

A boat was quickly manned and lowered. I hung at the rail, peering hard through the darkness. Below, Mr. Ringrose took a stance at the bow and held a lantern aloft to throw a light over the waters. While I felt no esteem for the three fallen pirates, or any man aboard this ship, I was filled with the seaman's dread of being lost in the deep.

Soon the longboat was at some distance, the lantern bobbing on the sea like a will-o'-the-wisp. As the *Bloody Hand* tacked about in the wind, every man aboard seemed to have his ear tuned to the darkness, listening for some faint cry for help.

Soon dawn broke over the horizon, like a great fire advancing across the seas. The longboat returned to the ship. "Not a sign of the poor ones," said Mr. Ringrose.

"Aye," the captain nodded. "From the look of it they went to the bottom like stones."

"A few words might be fittin', Capting."

"A few words they'll get," answered Captain Scratch. "Bare your heads, shipmates."

Everyone gathered around, but with the skull and crossbones dancing from the masthead, and with the captain's devilish red beard flying in the wind, the oration seemed more frump than piety.

"Lord," he said, "I commend to Ye our three brave comrades. Tender-hearts they were, aye, and honest to a fault. We'll miss their happy faces, Sir. Never did an evil thought cross their minds but what they struggled with it to the best of their abilities. They'll serve Ye well in the heavenly foc'sle, Sir. But if Ye chart them a course in the other direction—why, I fancy they'll find a few old swabs to sit around the fire with, and be not too sulky about the lodgings. Amen. Helmsman! Come about on course!"

The matter was at an end.

Or so I thought until midmorning when the bo'sun piped all hands. Even the lookout was called down from the masthead to line up on the quarterdeck. The day was now dazzling to the eye and the planking hot underfoot.

I stood at the end of the line, with Jibboom winding around my legs. When the captain appeared, a deep glow in his eyes, I had a foreboding that the day's troubles were not over.

He passed before us with Mr. Ringrose at his elbow, the both of them making a count of our noses. They reversed course and counted us again, muttering the numbers to themselves. A solemn, bad-weather look passed between them. Now the captain began to pace back and forth, sunk in thought. "Devilish," he muttered.

"Aye, devilish," echoed the first mate.

Meanwhile, so it seemed to me, these pirates were not unduly saddened by the loss of their comrades. It meant that Gentleman Jack's treasure could be cut up into larger shares.

"Shipmates," Captain Scratch said finally, tugging at his

beard. "A most grievous condition now exists aboard the *Bloody Hand*."

"Aye, a grievous condition," echoed the first mate.

"We live by our wits, maties, eh? Our wits and a sea chest full of luck. The smile of fortune! Is there a man standing before me who wouldn't be dancing under the gallows without it?"

"Aye, luck and more luck," mumbled the first mate.

"And I say our luck has fouled this morning, me tender-hearts! By the loss of three shipmates, may their timbers rest in peace, we are now a company of—" and here he seemed almost to choke on the words "—*of thirteen men*! Aye, that black and devilish number—*thirteen!*"

It was as if, for a moment, the sun itself had darkened. The buccaneers traded quick glances. For my part, I was not greatly discomfited. While I was not overly fond of that number, I was not overly skittish about it, either.

"Thirteen of us, by a tally of noses," the captain growled. "It blights this voyage, I say. It sets our luck adrift! Does a man stand before me who would continue the voyage under this black omen? Let him step forward."

Not a man made a move.

"Aye, it sets a cloud over us, shipmates. For an hour I and Mr. Ringrose have put our skulls to the problem. Shall we scuttle the venture, I ask ye? Shall we let those golden chests rot in the sand? Nay, do ye say? Agreed! Hear me, lads—there remains but one course open to us. We must reduce our number to twelve."

This announcement was followed by a glowering silence.

"Scuttle the voyage or scuttle a man, say I," the captain declared. "Do I hear ayes or nays?"

I could barely believe my ears. Was Captain Scratch proposing to pitch a man overboard?

"Aye," said Big Nose Ned. "Scuttle a man—that's my vote."

"Aye," said Cannibal, with a great shrug.

"Aye," said Hajji, the Red Sea sailor, giving his ragged moustaches a twirl. "We'll be at the island soon, yes? Why take bad luck ashore, eh?"

"Nay!" Jack o' Lantern sang out heartily. "Nay, ye cursed pack of fools—begging yer pardon, Captain. *Nay,* say I. Why, thirteen's as jolly a number as any other, ye dim-witted mooncalves! I'll sail under it, for sure and certain I will!"

His sentiment produced only catcalls and charges of cowardice. I thought it a fine speech and full of courage. Jack o' Lantern, alone, was keeping his wits about him. The ayes burst out, one after the other along the line, and stopped short at me. The sun burned in my eyes like a firebrand. These sea robbers meant to scuttle their thirteenth fellow without delay. It was the blackest villainy, but they delighted in it. The odds against each buccaneer were long, and the treasure shares would fatten again.

"Nay," said I, to another burst of laughter.

"The boy's too young to have a vote," Mr. Ringrose chuckled.

"But not too young, *effendi,* to take his chances walking the plank," said Hajji, cocking a watery eye at me.

"Aye, he'll have to take his risks with the rest of us," Captain Scratch answered, giving me a sly wink. "We'll draw for the plank, fair and square. Every man equal, no quarter given. If the grommet draws bad luck, he's a Jonah—why it'll prove the point—and we'd best be rid of him, treasure or not."

I put no confidence in his scurvy wink. He was gambling on

the odds to favor me, I thought, and if they didn't there was always Billy Bombay. If I drew the plank, the plank it would be. And he had his own neck to worry about. If he drew bad luck he'd be out on the wrong end of the plank himself.

Now that the conditions were laid down the buccaneers regained their humor—in fact, they seemed eager to tempt their fates and gamble for their lives.

Captain Scratch pulled two leather money pouches from his sash, and held one in each hand. "I have counted six gold doubloons into one pouch and seven in the other—not wanting to put the thirteen coins together," he said. That seemed to strike everyone as a sensible measure. "A single coin, lads, have I marked with a cross. If ye fetch up the cross, ye get the plank. Twelve will win, aye, and only one the loser. Choose your sack and choose your coin. Reach in, me lads. If it's me that plucks the crossed doubloon and walks the plank, why, you'd do wise to choose Mr. Ringrose captain."

With that he passed along the assembled men, and one by one the hairy hands dove into a pouch. Hajji made all manner of strange signs before testing his luck. Ezra Fly wet his lips, peering from sack to sack, before raising the courage to pluck out a doubloon. No one looked. Every man made a tight fist around the coin in his hand and waited until all had chosen.

When the pouches drew near me my heart began to pound, and when they reached me it was drumming wildly.

"Lively, boy!" Captain Scratch said. "Be done with it."

There could be only three coins left, as there only remained the captain himself, Mr. Ringrose and myself. I put up the bravest front I could and, with my right hand, reached into a pouch. I made do with the first coin I touched and held out my fist, like the others.

Now Captain Scratch, with a merry twinkle rising in his eye, stood before the first mate. "Mr. Ringrose," he said. "Since ye may find yourself captain of this ship before the hour is out, I'll give ye a taste of the captain's privilege to be last. Hold the pouches, *Captain* Ringrose, and I'll make me choice. The final doubloon will be yours."

It seemed a handsome gesture and Mr. Ringrose sparked noticeably at being addressed as Captain. The two leather pouches were set in his bony hands. With hardly a moment's decision Captain Scratch came up with a doubloon in his fist. The last coin fell to Mr. Ringrose, and the pouches were thrown to the deck.

"All right, shipmates," Captain Scratch said. "We drew fair and square. Who walks the plank for the benefit of all? Open up, me lads."

Fingers, now trembling like worms, uncurled. Mr. Ringrose himself began to quake like jelly. I abhorred the feel of the coin in my hand. My fist turned to sweat. I was positive I had drawn the crossed doubloon. I couldn't make my fingers open.

And then there came a howl of voices at my left.

"There's the mark!"

"Aye! He's drawn it!"

"Jack o' Lantern!"

Thunder and lightning! Jack o' Lantern! Of all these beggars—he was the thirteenth man! He, who now struck me as the most valorous and worthy man aboard.

"Aye, buckos," said the unlucky man, as cool as you please. "It's me, for sure and certain."

I was so enormous sorry that I couldn't look at him. And in that moment I saw with fresh horror that Captain Scratch hadn't played it fair and square at all. With everyone now clustering around Jack o' Lantern, I spied Captain Scratch pluck a coin from his sash. Until that moment his fist had been empty!

There had been only *twelve* doubloons in the pouches.

I stood gaping. He had merely pretended to draw out a coin, and left the last one to Mr. Ringrose. No wonder a merry twinkle had danced in his eyes. He was not risking his neck with the rest of us.

But now, as he found my eyes on him, he gave me such a murderous glance in return that I knew it would cost me my life to open my mouth.

"Fetch a plank, lads!" he said.

"Aye."

A rough plank was quickly laid out over the bulwark. Jack o' Lantern took a last look about him at the blue sky and the white clouds. I had never seen a man face death with a bolder spirit. He would not beg these scoundrels for his life. He would die nobly, with a smile on his lips. But all the while, I thought, his mind was working away lickety-cut.

His head scarf was fastened around his eyes. There was so much burden to him that it took three men to hoist him to the plank. It was all I could do to keep my tongue still. If anyone deserved to walk the plank it was Captain Scratch, whose eyes never strayed from me. Now he drew his cutlass as if to chop in two any thought I gave voice to.

"Quick done is merciful done!" he roared.

Jack o' Lantern stretched out his arms for balance and the plank bent under him like a bow. He turned about slowly to face us. "Boys," he said, and the morning sun was ablaze on his face. "Gents, I leave yer company with a light heart. Aye, to consort with blockheads is to die like one. There's something to be said in favor of the plank. I'll be spared yer fate at the hangman's rope. But, lads, don't rub yer hands over me treasure share too quick—I ain't dead yet. Ye forgot the gold purse around me neck. Heavy it is, and will do me no good where I'm going. It belongs to the first man with courage enough to take it off me."

There was greed enough among these gents of the sea, but they would not be tricked. Even blindfolded at the end of a plank, Jack o' Lantern was a dangerous foe and not one of his fellows took a fancy to his gold. They were, in fact, so relieved not to be in his place that they began to urge him off the plank with pikes and muskets.

I had seen enough and turned away. In that moment I spied the merest speck on the horizon. It appeared so suddenly that I was almost too tongue-tied to speak. Then I yelled out.

"Land, ho! Land, ho!"

It brought the buccaneers up short and just in time. Hearing my shout, Jack o' Lantern began clinging to the end of the plank like a huge barnacle.

"Aye, land it is!" said Captain Scratch.

"Is it Gentleman Jack's island?"

"Not in these waters, lads. Why what ye see there ain't much more than a shoal, but it'll do." Then he made a gesture toward Jack o' Lantern. "Fetch him back, boys. No sense in letting that gold pouch go to the bottom. We'll maroon him in the bargain."

Within an hour we hove to off the island. It was a mere dune of sand rising from the sea. The longboat was lowered. Jack o' Lantern was rowed ashore with a small keg of water. His life was spared, but slow death faced him on the island. There wasn't so much as a tree for shade.

At the last moment his courage failed him and I watched as

Mr. Ringrose and Ezra Fly and Big Nose Ned carried him bodily ashore. And there he sat, along the rim of blinding white sand—a lone figure slumped against the water keg. We were far off the sea lanes and he knew he would perish. He didn't so much as give us a glance as we sailed away.

I watched until the island itself slipped behind the horizon.

CHAPTER 6

*In which it rains and rains
and rains and rains*

E XACTLY WHERE we stood off the Spanish Main I had
no idea. In the days that followed it became clear that
Captain Scratch was dubersome about the matter himself.

He made a show of coming out on deck with his brass sex-
tant. He'd take the sun's position and mutter, "Aye—right on
course, mates. Right on course." And then, almost in the same
breath, he would advise the helmsman to ease over a few points
on the compass. We sailed east and west and north and south—
sometimes all in a single day. He had overshot the island.

He took to pacing the deck at night, squinting furiously at
the stars as if they made a liar of the compass. At this date, by
his own calculations, every man aboard ought to be running his
hands through gold and jewels—"Aye, up to your elbows in the
stuff, lads!"

Still, there were signs of land to be read in the endless sea.
Late one afternoon a coconut floated by. The next day the look-

out spied the glimmer of an island—but it turned out to be a drifting tangle of branches and tree roots. As we bore down on it, a dozen birds rose up in squawking circles, as if they were laughing at us.

And then the weather closed in. The stars clouded over, the wind rose from the southwest, and with it came rain. It rained infernally. It rained unending. The canvas flapped and cracked like wet sheets on a line. Rain filled the longboat. Rain danced on the decks and rushed away through the scuppers. We went wandering over the seas like a half-drowned dog trying to find its way home. Clearly, we were lost.

"Right on course, me hearties. Aye—steady as ye go." Captain Scratch was like a man talking to himself, and his fellow pirates began throwing him dark, side-long glances. His navigation was as crooked as a log fence and we might be a thousand miles off course.

Mr. Ringrose was quick to see an opportunity for advancement. "He'll fetch us up at the South Pole, maties," I heard him grumble. "Why, I could chart a better course with my head in a tar barrel."

Captain Scratch had made a mistake in addressing him as *Captain* Ringrose, and it had whet his appetite. He took such a fancy to the title that his quick, lurching walk altered to a measured, deliberate pace, with one arm carried thoughtfully behind his back. In rags though he was, he put on the airs of an admiral. Now as Captain Scratch kept more and more to his cabin, Mr. Ringrose grew more and more bold in his commands.

As the ship was shorthanded, he used me on the bottom sails when the captain wasn't about. My hair had grown long and lanky and I tarred myself a pigtail to keep it back out of my eyes. Wouldn't Aunt Katy have a fit to see me with tar in my hair and dancing along a footrope!

I was put to standing two-hour watches at the wheel when the wind was slack. I could feel the sea itself in my hands—the current tugging to wrest the helm from me. The warm rain showered down, my boots never dried out, but I was chirk and happy at these duties. The cooper's trade was not for me—no, sir. I'd keep an eye fixed on the compass and forget this was an outlaw ship under my feet. She was a whaler and we were out in the far oceans hunting blubber.

As food grew short I'd catch Cannibal looking at me in a strange way, which did provide me with some uneasy moments. Food grew shorter still. I was soon hungry from the time I rose in the morning until I turned in at night. We were reduced to a midday bowl of pease soup with a chunk of moldy potato in it. Bugs and weevils floated on top, which I was careful to skim off, but the others about me were not so fussy as to give up these bitter morsels.

The air below decks turned foul and pestiferous with fumes from the bilge. I believe the rats would have left us if they could have found a way off the ship. Big Nose Ned, whose sense of smell was touchy, tried to fumigate by filling an iron pot with gunpowder and vinegar, and dropping in red-hot bars. The vapors that arose were almost as foul as before.

And still the weather failed to clear. It was as if the storm was following us around, and Mr. Ringrose took it as a sign that the captain had used up his luck. Tempers were short and mischief was brewing for sure. There had been mischief enough on this voyage, and I tried not to think of Jack o' Lantern marooned and his bones bleaching in the sun. He was no doubt many days dead.

Trouble came to a head just after daybreak when Mr. Ringrose removed his arm from behind his back and ordered me aloft. The lookout stood two-hour watches and there were hardly enough men to go around. I was glad enough to take the watch and crawled up the ratlines to the crow's nest. I set my legs against the pitch and sway of the mast. Through the downpour I could barely see a ship's length beyond the bows, but I kept my eyes peeled.

When Captain Scratch came out on deck and spied me at the masthead he flew into a rage.

"Who sent ye aloft, boy!" he shouted.

Mr. Ringrose came around the deck house and answered for me. The two pirates began to roar and wave their arms about. Again Captain Scratch called up to me.

"Down with ye!"

"Stay!" shouted Mr. Ringrose.

The captain turned on him and exploded. "Ye scurvy-necked, bilge-headed fool!" Then to me again. "Avast! Down with ye!"

"Avast! Stay with ye!"

At this further impertinence Captain Scratch drew his cutlass. The crew came running from all quarters of the ship. I lost most of the words in the rain, but the matter under discussion was clear enough from the posturings below. And then, like a clap of thunder, I heard Captain Scratch roar out, "It's *captain* you'll be is it? When I finish with ye, ye won't be fit for cabin boy!"

Mr. Ringrose assumed all his airs, arm behind his back. I heard the words "elect . . . laws of the old brethren . . ."

"Aye—I'll elect ye on the point of this blade!"

Hajji threw Mr. Ringrose a pike and the two buccaneers backed off. Before many more moments passed it seemed to me our number would be reduced to eleven.

"Lay on, ye scrawny, keel-nosed jailbird!" Captain Scratch boomed.

The two men clashed like grim death. There was a clanking of weapons in the rain. Some impulse led me to look up, and in that moment, I saw a dark green shape loom up. I didn't hold my tongue even for an instant.

"Land ho!" I yelled through my hands. "Dead ahead! Dead ahead!"

The shout turned the two combatants to stone.

"It's Gentleman Jack's!" cried Captain Scratch.

"Aye!" answered John Ringrose. "And yer runnin' us aground!"

CHAPTER 7

*We scrape bottom and I crawl
under the shell of a turtle*

CANNIBAL, STANDING the helm watch, spun the wheel spokes into a blur. The ship groaned in all its joints, the bowsprit swung about, and the two combatants on deck were hurled into each other's arms.

The sea cliff seemed to race toward us through the rain. We were almost beam to now—so close that I thought I could reach out and touch land.

"To starboard!" the captain cried. "Hard over—hard over!"

By that time three sailors had thrown themselves against the wheel, but too late. We were scraping bottom. There was a deep crunching sound from below. The rigging shook, the crosstrees swayed, and lines snapped and went lashing through the air. I wrapped my arms around the masthead and held on.

But our own seaway carried us free. We went grinding past the headland itself only to find ourselves broaching to toward a shallow cove with a steep black rim of beach. Here an ocean swell caught us broadside and, tossing us like a chip of wood, drove us into the sand. I was almost whipped off the mast. We landed on our beam ends, high and dry, like a beached whale.

The ship settled with a creaking and sighing of timbers, and now the surf broke around the hull with hissing sounds. If the *Bloody Hand* was stove in I reckoned on spending the next hundred years on this out-of-the-way island. Maybe longer.

I was shaken from this thought by the roaring voice of Captain Scratch from the slanting deck below. Despite the downpour of rain he was suddenly in the sunniest of spirits—he was, in fact, laughing wildly. With one leg planted against the sternpost, he was flashing his cutlass at the crew.

"Didn't I tell ye!" he shouted. "Right on course! Aye, *exactly* on course! Did ye doubt Harry Scratch, ye swivel-eyed, mutinous scum! Lent an ear to John Ringrose, did ye—John, who couldn't navigate a mud puddle on a clear day. It's a new captain ye want, is it? Aye—I'll resign me office, ye bellyaching turnips. You'll get no help from me in filling your pockets with gold! Set your own course, ye bunch of cabbages, and me and Oliver Finch'll set ours. Aye! I'll give ye John Ringrose with me best compliments, lads—and I guarantee he'll navigate ye straight to the gallows!"

There was a quick protest from the crew, somehow like the barking of seals. "Nay! Nay!" came the shouts, one on the other.

"You're cap'n, Cap'n!"

"Aye—any man who says not will answer to me, *effendi,*" snarled Hajji, who only a few moments before was clearly on John Ringrose's side.

Ringrose, meanwhile, was cowering along the taffrail and try-ing to make himself invisible. He was quaking so that I fancied I could almost hear his bones rattling. Hajji caught him by the leg and pulled him loose, and shouting like savages the others joined in. They were quick to blame him for their own muti-nous grumblings and I thought they would tear him apart.

"Belay that!" shouted Captain Scratch. "If it's me that's in command, it's me that'll set the punishment—time and place! Drop him, lads."

The sailors were quick to comply. As they had Ringrose up by the feet they dropped him on his head. It seemed to cause him no great discomfort. He scurried out of reach and even passed Captain Scratch a groveling salute. "Thank ye, Capting," he croaked. "Yer ol' shipmate John Ringrose meant ye no harm—strike me ugly if I did. Let bygones be bygones, I say. Why, Drake himself could have run aground in weather like this."

"Aground, do ye say!" Captain Scratch laughed. "Aground! *Careened*, ye mean. Aye, heeled over as gentle as ye please. Ca-reen ship and scrape, that's the order. The hull is growing sea grass like a beard and barnacles by the ton! Do ye think I'd sail another league so slow in the water we couldn't overtake a tur-tle boat, eh? Is it any wonder we're overdue here at Gentleman Jack's, dragging all that sea slop with us? Ye call yourselves sail-ors? Aground, do ye call it? *Careened*, I say! Cannibal, break out the scraping irons!"

Standing in the billowing rain the crew didn't take to this command with any show of eagerness. "Do you mean to scrape the hull now?" said one of the buccaneers. "In this foul weather, Cap'n?"

"Well now, *I* don't mean to scrape at all. *I* intend to go ashore. Grommet!"

"Aye," I shouted, starting down the slanting mast by the seat of my breeches. I was anxious to go ashore myself—the sooner the better.

"Avast, lad. I promote ye to me personal advisor. How does that suit ye? It's John Ringrose I'm calling. Cabin boy!"

"Aye," Ringrose piped up meekly, and I was monstrous sorry to see him so humbled.

"Hackle me bones, how the mighty has fallen! Over the side with ye and scrape. There's the ticket for ye! Chip away at them barnacles, ye sniveling bilge rat. Scrape away at that sea grass. Lay to until your hands is raw and your back is stove in. And when you've got the hull as clean as an eggshell, why we'll careen again—and ye can scrape the other side. Lay to, ye mutineering sack of bones—lay to!"

The tide ebbed away, leaving the *Bloody Hand* almost entirely out of water. Captain Scratch had three cannons moved ashore, their muzzles pointing seaward, in the event that we were surprised in the cove. Then he had canvas rigged for shelter and a hammock strung between two palm trees. They grew like upturned feather dusters. I had never seen these trees before, although my father had once described them to me, and I suppose I stood gaping at the wonder of them.

"Close your mouth, boy," said Captain Scratch. "You'll catch mosquitoes." He wrung out his beard, hoisted himself into the sheltered hammock, and folded his hands across his stomach. He was going to sleep out the bad weather. "There'll be no ghosting until night falls, lad, and maybe not even then. Gentleman Jack was never one to go sloshing about in the rain."

Soon he was snoring and John Ringrose could be heard chipping and banging away at the hull. He didn't seem to mind the labor—in fact, he seemed content to be getting off so light. Meanwhile, the pirates went leaping into the jungle to hunt fresh food. I wandered off by myself, soaked to the skin, but suddenly free of Captain Scratch, Hajji, Cannibal and the others. I could escape. Escape to where?

I stumbled into a large rock, which turned out to be the empty shell of a large sea turtle. I curled myself up under it, snug and dry. After a moment I heard a scratching sound and lifted the edge of the shell to let Jibboom in. He curled up beside me like a wet rag and we listened to the rattle of rain on the shell. There was nowhere to escape to, and I wondered if I would ever see my father and Aunt Katy and Nantucket again.

I didn't know I had fallen asleep until I woke up. The rain had stopped. I listened to a sound of muffled voices nearby. I lifted the edge of the shell and peered out. There, not thirty feet away, sat Hajji and Cannibal and several other buccaneers with a wild boar spitted over an open fire. The meat fats were dripping and popping in the flames. I was starved. The rich, juicy odors went to the pit of my hollow stomach. But I held back. The pirates were laughing among themselves and a cask of rum passed from man to man.

"I don't see where *he* comes in for a full share," I heard one of the sailors growl.

"Aye," echoed another.

I couldn't make out who they were talking about, but then Hajji bared his sharp teeth in a grin and matters became clear enough. "Don't worry about the young dog," he said, his shoe-leather face glistening. "Do you take the captain for a fool, eh, *effendi*?" Once we get our hands on that gold, thanks be to Allah—what need have we of the boy?" He curled his moustaches and laughed. "By the beard of the Prophet, I know that devil we call captain. Aye, when we're ready to sail—he'll leave the young dog behind!"

CHAPTER 8

*In which I am taken by
surprisal, and what
happened next*

THE HAIR shot up on my neck. With my heart clatter-wacking so loud I thought they would hear it, I lowered the turtle shell. I was to be marooned! Left to perish like Jack o' Lantern!

Here was a black and plaguey greeting to Gentleman Jack's island! I felt the anger in my eyes like sparks. Was there ever such a double-faced scoundrel as Captain Scratch? I'd gladly see him hung in chains! He meant to trick me, did he?

Not if I kept my wits about me. That ghost wasn't spied out yet. That treasure wasn't dug up, either. I was one against them all. Two, counting Jibboom. We'd run off and hide. Let Captain Scratch and his scurvy pack of cutthroats try to find those moldering treasure boxes without me. Why, they'd come begging me to point out the spot, and I wouldn't even then. No, sir! Not until I had some way to get myself off the island.

By thunder, I had the advantage of them and I'd make the most of it. I peered again at the crew waiting around the beach fire for the wild boar to roast. Again the rich odors came to me and I was seized by such a hunger that I almost put off running away. But finally I began backing off, shell, Jibboom and all. I don't think I covered ten feet in ten minutes. I moved like a snail, only not as fast. My empty stomach got to growling so noisily I thought it would give me away.

It seemed an hour before I found myself deep among long tufts of beach grass. And then, so suddenly that for a moment I froze on the spot, the shell was ripped off my back. I thought it must be Hajji or Cannibal or one of the others, but it wasn't. When I looked up I saw a dead man standing over me.

It was Jack o' Lantern!

Before I could open my mouth to gasp, he clamped a pudgy hand across my face. "Not a sound, bucko!" he whispered. He wore a dirty scarf around his head and a knife in his belt. His round, grinning face was pale as death. It was an apparition!

The sweat popped out on my forehead. Jack o' Lantern had perished. I had seen him left to die of hunger and thirst on a sand speck in the boundless sea. He couldn't be before me now in the mortal flesh. I had raised a ghost in broad daylight! Didn't Captain Scratch himself believe I had the dark power?

"Steady, shipmate," he chuckled softly, bending his face closer to mine. My hair must have surely been standing on end. I thought Jibboom would spit at him—but, of course, that be-fuddled cat couldn't *see* him. "Steady. It's no castaway spook yer looking at. I'm alive—for sure and certain I am."

« *61*

I could feel his breath close against my face. I gazed into his pale blue eyes, and he gave me a fat wink. And then, like a sharp blow, my senses returned. He was no daylight ghost. The first sight of him had sent my mind spinning. Jack o' Lantern was flesh and blood! His touch was warm and Jibboom was rubbing his back against his leg.

Seeing that my alarm had passed, he released his hand from my mouth. The question in my mind now reached the bursting point.

"But how—"

He crossed his lips with a thick finger to silence me. "Later. Let's slip anchor before they get wind of us, bucko. Follow me."

He gazed around to make sure the way was clear and then led me at a crouch to deep cover. The sun, breaking through the clouds, was raising steam from the island jungle. We were soon swallowed up in a leafy gloom of growing things—banana trees in clumps, coconut palms and crab-lemon trees in great prickly clouds. There was a chittering of birds, and now and then the cry of a wild parrot high in some tree.

Jack o' Lantern seemed to know his way about the island and steered his course without hesitation. I was hardly able to keep up with him. He was as swift and light on his feet as a ball bouncing away ahead of me. We scampered over broken boulders and leaped rivulets of rainwater draining off into the sea. And we climbed. At our approach a flock of plump pigeons broke out of the ground steam and went clattering through the dazzling shafts of sunlight.

We reached a high sea cliff and here Jack o' Lantern stopped. He was breathing heavily, but smiling. He spread the low-hanging leaves of a banana tree and we gazed below at the ship heeled over with John Ringrose chipping away at the hull. Smoke was rising from the beach where the pirate crew waited on the spitted boar. At this distance their revelry and laughter were soundless.

Jack o' Lantern drew his knife and cut a hanging stalk of red bananas. My stomach was thundering, but I didn't know how to go about eating a banana—never having met one before, except by hearsay.

"Now we'll have us a feast and a talk," said Jack o' Lantern, leaning his back against the nearest tree trunk. He ripped a banana off the stalk and I did the same. It felt heavy and rubbery and none too appetizing. I took a bite anyway, not being in a particular mood. Jack o' Lantern gazed at me and then broke into a quiet laugh. "It needs peeling, bucko!"

I spit out what I had in my mouth and watched him skin one down to the fruit inside. That was all the banana education I needed. The inside was sweet and filling and there was plenty more. I went at the stalk full chisel.

"So ye know the worst of it, do ye, shipmate?" he said finally. "The captain figures to maroon ye."

"You heard them talking?" I asked. Again, I was seized with the wonder of his being here on this island.

"Aye."

"But how—"

He tore off another banana. "Well, now, myself was hid in the grass as ye came turtling by. Almost ran me down, ye did. Unless I mistake ye, it's in yer mind to scamper off from our shipmates, eh?"

I nodded with my mouth full, and swallowed. "Yes, sir."

The vapors were rising all about us as if we had taken seats on the smoky outskirts of Hades. "That won't do," he chuckled.

"Not a bit, it won't. Why, a one-legged man could walk around this island in half a day. There's no snug hiding place for ye."

"I'll find myself one," I said.

He bent forward and grinned. "Are we friends? Aye, friends unless proved otherwise, eh? Then listen to yer friend Jack o' Lantern, who knows every pirate trick in the log. Myself, who has lived up as many lives as that cat—and enjoyed every one. I, who has made a fine study of the art of survival. Me, who tumbled out of the cradle and went adventuring. I'll be yer schoolmaster, bucko. I'll learn ye—and the first thing is to keep a laugh up yer sleeve for emergencies. And the next is not to do a thing hasty—like running off just for the mischief of it."

"I'm not going back."

"I mislike to tell ye this, shipmate, but yer going back if I have to deliver ye in person."

"No, sir," I said, clamping my jaws.

"*Aye.*" He moved a lump of banana to his other cheek like a cud of tobacco. "Do ye know what our good friend Captain Scratch will do when ye turn up missing?"

I wiped my lips on the back of my hand. "Let him try to whistle up that treasure without me."

"Aye, that's the very point. I'll tell ye what he'll do. He'll set Cannibal on yer scent—him with a nose like a bloodhound for human flesh. He'll smell ye out, bucko, and maybe take a slabbering bite out of yer leg if the captain ain't looking."

I was quick to imagine that Fiji savage trailing me and maybe even spitting me over a fire like the wild boar below. That was more imagination than the situation called for, but a cold shiver flashed down my back anyway. I couldn't run away. I had no fancy for Captain Scratch's company, and that left me between the fat and the fire.

"Now, don't give it such a long face," Jack o' Lantern chuckled. "We'll turn it to our advantage, for sure and certain, bucko. As for the captain—why, between us we'll fix his flint."

I was quiet for a long time and finally, when I lifted my eyes again, I said, "Jack o' Lantern, how did you get yourself on this island?"

"By jingo, there's a merry question," he smiled. "And the how of it makes a merry answer."

"The last I remember you were sitting alone in the sand. Then we clapped on a wind and left you behind."

"Aye."

"You looked grievous sad, sir."

"Aye."

"Your head was turned from us. You didn't even bother to look."

"For a fact I didn't. And for a fact, I couldn't."

"Couldn't?"

"That's the truth of it, bucko. It wasn't *myself* left sitting like a castaway."

I gaped at him. His round, grinning face in the rising steam made me wonder if my senses were sorely bewitched. "It wasn't you?" I muttered and understood nothing.

"I mean to say—it was myself and it wasn't."

"Was and wasn't?"

"Aye. I took no fancy to twiddling my thumbs on that salty speck of land, Oliver. I was difficulted to think of some way to save my neck, worthless as it is—except to me. Now listen close, for I mean to instruct ye, lad. If we know a thing about our shipmates it's this—every imp and devil aboard would trade his own mother for half her weight in gold bars."

I nodded. I could believe it.

"Aye, they wear their greed like a ring in the nose and ye can pull them around by it. Now, there enters another fact. I mislike to admit it to ye, but there is a terrible flaw in my character, Oliver—I have a streak of the honest. Aye. It has been a great embarrassment to me in the pursuit of my unlawful occasions. But honest I am, if given the choice, like my father before me, who was a cobbler. When I lay my word to a thing my shipmates know it won't be broke—in short, lad, they trust me, and there's a power in that."

Jibboom went high-stepping over his feet and leaped to the limb of a tree.

"Did I say it *was* and *wasn't* myself marooned?" Jack o' Lantern went on. "Aye. When they lowered me in the longboat for the island, there was John Ringrose, ye recall, together with Ezra Fly and Big Nose Ned. Not two ounces of brains between the three of them, but wise in the ways of blood and treasure. I told them what I'm telling ye now, that they'd never share-out Gentleman Jack's buried plunder—never. Not once Captain Scratch got his grappling hooks on it. I've made too many voyages with that crafty blackleg not to know the twists and turns of his mind."

He paused to lean closer and tap my arm with his finger. "Do ye know why he fears the dredgies will return for him in the black of night, with their wet footprints, eh? It's his old dead shipmates that fevers his mind. Aye, them that was along when Gentleman Jack was murdered and the plunder buried on this very island seven years ago. Within an hour after we sailed away he ran out the plank and sent them marching off the end of it, one by one. He wanted to be rid of them—aye, for the tales they might tell and because ye don't have to share-out with dead men. That's his policy. But that's what distempers his sleep, too—afraid, he is, that them dredgy shipmates will climb back out of the brine and catch him like a weasel asleep!"

"Were those the men who had helped bury the treasure?"

"Aye, the very ones. And once the treasure is aboard he'll run out the plank again. He'll sail the ship singlehanded before he'll part with so much as a gold button. So there in the longboat I looked John Ringrose in the eye and said—'John, ye'll be a dredgy yerself before this voyage ends. And the same goes for ye, Ezra Fly, and ye also, Big Nose Ned. I guarantee it. Ye have my word on it. He'll share-out with none of ye. By time ye sight London Town he'll scuttle the last man. But I have a plan to save yer necks and yer gold at the same time.' And John Ringrose looked at me while the others rowed and said to me what yer about to say, Oliver."

"A plan?" I muttered.

"Aye. The very word. A plan. 'Let me off the hook, boys,' I told them. 'I know how to catch that weasel asleep. Here's my word on it.' All the while I was talking I was sunk down in the sternsheets among the ropes and canvas, and slipping out of my clothes. I stuffed my pants and shirt with canvas, and wrapped my head scarf around some ropes—and that's what they carried ashore and set in the sand. Not me. My clothes. That's what ye saw from the taffrail, boy. I remained hid under canvas as they rowed back to the ship and when they hauled the longboat aboard I came with it. In the night I crept down to the ballast stones, and there I've been these two weeks, living in the dark and turning white as a ghost for ye. Once we beached I watched for my chance and slipped ashore—and that's the was and wasn't of it."

We fell silent. My mind ranged back to that forlorn figure seated in the sand—a buccaneer stuffed with canvas and a hank of rope for a head. By thunder, Jack o' Lantern was a man to reckon with, as cunning and crafty as Captain Scratch himself.

Finally I said, "What is your plan, Jack o' Lantern?"

"Why, simple it is, bucko," he grinned. "I'm going to clap the knave out of Captain Scratch and turn him into an honest man."

CHAPTER 9

In which time passes,
most of it at night

I SUPPOSE my eyebrows shot up several inches. Captain
Scratch with the knave clapped out of him! That would be
a grandacious thing to witness, but how Jack o' Lantern expected to perform such a feat I couldn't guess—and he
wouldn't say. He merely chuckled and gave me a wink.

"The first thing to set our talents to is that treasure, me fine
young bucko," he said. "Aye, we've got to dredge it up behind
the captain's back. Are ye with me? Will ye do as I say?"

"I will," I answered, eager to serve in this enterprise and
hugely pleased to have Jack o' Lantern as a friend.

"Then back ye go. When it falls dark the captain will take ye
tramping for a glimpse of Gentleman Jack. Ye'll keep yer
weather eye peeled. But if ye fetch him up, lad—keep a quiet
tongue in yer head. Can ye do that?"

I didn't answer. I wasn't sure but what a look at that

sleeveless ghost might raise the hair on my scalp and set my bones to rattling.

"Do ye hear?"

"Yes, sir."

"Aye, mum's the word. Ye won't give a sign to Captain Scratch. Ye won't let on. Just go about yer ghosthunting, but ground-mark the spot with yer knife. I'll find it. Myself will root up that plunder and together we'll give the captain such a surprise that the fire will fly out of his eyes like live coals!"

"But what if I can't *see* ghosts?"

"Ye were born the same as Billy Bombay, weren't ye?"

"Yes."

"Well, he has the eye for 'em. Why, I remember once, during the dark of the moon, we went ashore in the tobacco colonies and without realizing it we cut across a cemetery and he told me the phantom gentry was up in such numbers that he could read a newspaper by the light they was giving off."

"But I've never spied a ghost," I said. "Not one."

"There's always a first time, bucko. I never seen the king of England, either, but if I was fetched up at Buckingham Palace, I reckon I'd see him clear enough. Maybe ye've never been on good ghosting grounds before. Aye, it's a dark business, but yer the lad for it."

I began to dread the coming of night.

It was late afternoon, with the sky blazing red, when I made my way back to Captain Scratch and the others. Jack o' Lantern told me not to worry—he'd be around. The last I saw of him he went bounding away through the tangled green foliage.

Even with the sun lowering, the island continued to steam like a chowder kettle. When I reached the beach the buccaneers were tearing at the roasted boar like a pack of hungry savages. Knives and cutlasses flashed, and there was a festive outcry. When Captain Scratch saw me his left cheek was swelled out like a cannonball and the meat fats were running down his beard.

"Avast, if it ain't young Oliver," he laughed. "Brooding about home, I fancy. I figured the smell of food would finally smoke ye out."

With that he lopped off a chunk of meat and spiked it with his cutlass. "Good health to ye."

"I'm not hungry," I said.

"Eat, boy! It'll take the home-fever out of ye. Why, you'll be walking down the wharf at Nantucket before ye grow another quarter of an inch. The devil seize me soul if I break me word on it!"

His word, indeed!

He flung the meat at me, and turned his attention to the sky. "Aye, it'll be dark soon enough. It wouldn't surprise me if we hauled up them gold boxes afore breakfast."

The others perked up at this and Hajji gave me a sly laugh. He knew what was in store for me, did he? Well, sir, I had a laugh waiting up *my* sleeve.

I got out my jackknife and carved off some meat for Jibboom. I found that I wasn't so full of red bananas that I couldn't stow away the warm-smelling roast boar. Meanwhile, I spied out Ezra Fly, who was licking his fingers, and Big Nose Ned. Little did they know that I was in league with Jack o' Lantern, the same as they were. John Ringrose had left his scraping irons and held a rib bone between his hands like a slice of watermelon. He had worked up a huge appetite.

And then Captain Scratch looked about him with a kind of

horrified wonder at the way his crew was going at their food. "Look at ye!" he said. "Gulching down your victuals like dogs! You're rich gentlemen-to-be, boys, and a gent eats his grub polite and grand-like—off the blade of his knife."

In no time at all, it seemed, the wild boar was a thing of bones. And then Captain Scratch, who fancied himself a gentleman, rubbed the fat drippings over his face and neck so that his skin shone fiercely. The others followed suit and I was soon to regret that I had not done the same.

The horizon swallowed the burning red sun. In these latitudes night came like a candle snuffed out. It fell dark very fast. Captain Scratch lit a ship's lantern and then directed Cannibal and Ezra Fly to shoulder digging spades.

Then he fixed me with his amber gaze. "Lead the way, me tender-heart. But mind, keep your wits about ye. If ye clap an eye on the ghost, cry out! Are ye ready, lad?"

"Yes, sir," I answered—determined that if the sulphurous one should leap out at me I wouldn't so much as blink my eyes.

"Then lay on."

And forward we marched, plunging single file into the trees. I led the way and Captain Scratch, a step behind me, swung the lantern, turned low, at his feet. "To watch for serpents," he explained, although Jack o' Lantern had told me there were no poisonous snakes on the island. It was the pitch dark Captain Scratch was afraid of, I recalled, and now that a heavy darkness was upon us I wasn't overly fond of it myself. Ezra Fly followed the captain and Cannibal took up the rear.

From time to time Captain Scratch advised me to make a tack to port or starboard, but mostly I followed my nose. We moved stealthily, as if to catch Gentleman Jack unaware. But now that night had fallen the jungle seemed to rouse from a slumber. The air came alive with the hum and whine of insects. Crickets were as thick as fleas. As we advanced, step by step, they burst with noise, tolling our way with a shrill ringing.

"Blast them *grillones*," the captain whispered, giving them, as I supposed, their Spanish name. "They're big as frogs on the Spanish Main and twice as noisy."

Clouds of gnats and mosquitoes discovered us and followed us along. I was kept busy fending them from my face. I was so hugely tormented that finally I snapped off a tree branch to fan them away.

Captain Scratch lifted the lantern to see what I was about. "Do ye spy him, lad?" he whispered.

"No, sir."

"Then what ails ye?"

"I'm eaten alive."

"Aye, the buggers!" he chuckled. Moths had gathered about the lantern in such numbers as almost to shut out the light. "They'll board and fight if ye don't know what you're about, matey. There ain't a pirate in these latitudes that don't know how to anoint himself."

"With what?"

"Hog fat! Aye, that puts an end to their close-quarter fighting." He rapped the lantern against his foot to knock it free of insects, but they swarmed again. "Lay on, matey."

Here and there a lightning bug shone like a star in the bushes. We tramped around for hours and I kept switching the insects from my face. We stopped now and again to look all about us.

"Do ye see him, lad? The merest glimpse, eh? The merest glimpse!"

"No, sir."

"Oh, he's a wiley one, is Gentleman Jack. He knows what we're about, I fancy, and will lead us a merry chase."

At one point, when we were resting, there was a great outcry of crickets at a slight distance, and Captain Scratch leaped to his feet.

"It's him! Aye, I can almost sniff brimstone on the air!"

We went crashing through the leaves and creepers as if to catch a rabbit by the leg.

"Look lively, boy!"

My heart was racing, but I steeled myself in the event the island phantom popped out at me. By thunder, I'd hold my tongue even if he breathed fire like a dragon. But ten minutes passed without catching sight of him. We came to a standstill. Captain Scratch bent close to whisper in my ear. "Here now, I'll give ye a leg up this tree. Look about ye. Ye may spy him lurking about the bushes."

I was soon aloft, climbing from limb to limb in a cedar-smelling tree. I found a high perch and settled myself. I gazed all around at the darkness below and slowly became aware that I was not alone in the tree.

There was a man on the next limb!

My scalp bristled. I very nearly cried out. But I had so set myself against surprisal that I didn't make a sound. If that was Gentleman Jack, he had no glow to him at all! I stared at the dark shape an arm's length away, and began to back down the tree.

"Bucko."

I stopped. What a monstrous fool I was! It was Jack o' Lantern.

"A good evening to ye," he whispered. "I warned ye I'd be about to keep an eye on the ghosting."

"Sh-h-h," I murmured. "They'll hear you below."

"Not with the *grillones* chirping and singing in their ears. Almost give me away, didn't they? Hot and thirsty, are ye, lad?"

"Aye," I answered.

He rummaged in his pockets and handed me something that felt like a small cannonball soft enough to eat. "A man can live off the land in these isles. It's off a genipa tree. Juicy. It'll refresh ye, bucko."

It *was* juicy, and full of sharp little pips. I went at it too eagerly, with the result that I got more juice down my shirt than down my throat.

Captain Scratch grew impatient at my silence and finally shouted up in a hushed voice. "Do ye sight him, matey!"

"No, sir!" I called back.

"Look sharp!"

I must have spent twenty minutes in the tree with Jack o' Lantern. He told me that the only fruit to beware of was the manchineel apple, which was poisonous. He knew a grist of things like that.

We crossed the island, and as the hours passed Captain Scratch's impatience turned to foul temper. He kept me on my feet until I thought I must be walking in my sleep and had hardly the energy to switch the gnats and mosquitoes off my face. He was forever imagining a whiff of brimstone on the air, which would send us flying off in a new direction. The night seemed endless, but when dawn broke without a glimpse of Gentleman Jack, Captain Scratch was in a wild-eyed fury. He shook a threatening fist at the jungle and roared, "Aye, we've got ye on the run, ye mildewed, worm-eaten ghost! Ye can look for us tomorrow night! We'll be back!"

We were a ragged-looking bunch when we came trooping down to the cove and the ship. The men lay asleep on the beach, scattered like driftwood. Captain Scratch kicked them awake, one by one.

"Rise and shine, ye lazy dogs!"

I noticed now that the front of my shirt was stained black by the dripping genipa fruit—it looked, in fact, as if fat jungle grasshoppers had spit at me in the night.

And then I saw that Captain Scratch was scowling at me. Did he wonder how I had got myself so spotted? He shut one eye suspiciously. I tried to get an answer ready, but I could hardly think, so bothered was I by a stinging and swelling of my face, and a blistering of my lips.

He strode closer and then stopped short. He was taking a good look at me in the daylight—not at my stained shirt, but at the branch I was using to fan away insects. And now his eyebrows all but flew off his face.

"Drop it!" he roared, as if I had a live serpent in my hand. "Manchineel, lad! It's manchineel!"

CHAPTER 10

Being a full account of
how I came to be strung up
by the ankles

MY FACE swelled up like a pumpkin. I was blind for three days. My skin felt in flames. My hand, too, was scalded where I had held the venomous manchineel branch.

With my eyes puffed shut the ghost hunt was at a standstill. Captain Scratch snarled and growled at the delay, and flayed the crew with his temper. "Blast ye for lazy swine!" he thundered, and ordered them one by one to the ship's hull. "Scrape and caulk, ye jimberjawed apes! Scrape and caulk!"

All day long the cove echoed with the pound and scrape of irons. I lay on the beach, protected from the burning sun by a shelter Ezra Fly had rigged up of palm branches. During the slow feverish hours my mind kept returning to Aunt Katy and my father and the worry I must be causing. It would be a wondrous thing if I ever saw home again.

I dozed, and I dreamed I was a cooper and that I clapped Captain Scratch in a barrel and rolled him down the cobbles to the High Lord of the Admiralty, who took a pinch of snuff and thanked me grandly. But then I awoke and the High Lord of the Admiralty disappeared and in his place I heard Captain Scratch call for a musket.

"There's boar enough on this island to victual the ship for a year. Cannibal! Follow me!"

Throughout the afternoon I heard musket fire in the jungle, and each shot raised Jack o' Lantern before my sightless eyes. I fully expected him to be brought in with his hands and feet triced to a bamboo pole.

By evening of the second day, however, they had not flushed Jack o' Lantern out of the greenery. But the captain's marksmanship was unerring. Five boar were hauled out of the jungle, skinned and salted and packed in barrels of brine.

That night I heard the men complain that the hull was so eaten by sea worms that certain spots were as thin as Spanish lace.

"Why, Capting," said John Ringrose. "There are planks I can poke my thumb through."

"Patch 'em with tar and oakum."

"Sir," Big Nose Ned put in, "that hull ain't fit for sea without new timbers. It's the sea grass that has been holding the ship together."

"Tar and oakum, I say!" answered the captain. "And if ye feel stomachy about sailing with us—why, you're welcome to the island after we're gone. Ha! Tar and oakum will do, lads, until we've hauled that treasure aboard. Aye, and then we'll seize us a smart ship and make a grand sight when we drop our mud-hook in the Thames!"

On the third day of my blindness I dozed through the worst heat of the day and awoke to a silence. The bang and scrape of ship's work had disappeared. Not a voice broke the stillness of the cove. There was only the rush of the surf against the beach, and suddenly I sat bolt upright.

The men were gone. I was alone.

I lurched blindly to my feet. Thunder and lightning, had they somehow dredged up the treasure without me and set sail? Was I marooned?

"Captain Scratch!"

I stumbled through the sand with my hands stretched out before me. I tried to see, but my swollen eyes remained as tightly closed as walnuts.

"Captain Scratch! Mr. Ringrose!"

And then, at some distance behind me, a voice answered. "Easy, bucko!"

Jack o' Lantern. I swung around. "Are they gone? Are we marooned?"

"Nay, lad. They refloated the ship. They'll bring her around to careen again and scrape the port side."

What a muddle-head I was! That was it, of course, and I gave a quick sigh of relief.

Jack o' Lantern told me that he was hiding in the beach grass, and I tried to follow the sound of his voice.

"What's happened to ye, bucko? Can't ye see?"

"No, sir." And I explained about the poison branch.

He clucked his tongue. "Aye, yer face is puffed up like a

blowfish. But it'll pass. For sure and certain, it will. Avast! The ship is heading in."

And he was gone.

When I awoke the following morning, my eyelids parted. I could see. The ship lay heeled over on its starboard side and throughout the day the men swung along the hull on lines from above, like spiders.

My recovery put a gleam in Captain Scratch's eye. He was chirk and lively. I had never seen him in better spirits. "Tonight, lad—I can feel it in me bones. Tonight, matey, we'll put salt on Gentleman Jack's tail feathers!"

During the day I washed out my shirt and hung it over a bush to dry. But the dark spots remained, black as pitch. When night fell Captain Scratch clapped me on the shoulder and we made another ghost-hunting foray into the jungle. By morning he was in a fury. We tried the next night and the next, but if Gentleman Jack poked his head above ground—I didn't see him.

Dark glances shot my way. The buccaneers were getting dubersome about my ghosting power, and I felt a mortal disappointment in myself. Maybe I had no such power! Or maybe I hadn't been born at the stroke of midnight as I had always been told.

The bottom work came to an end and the ship was refloated on the high tide. We moved back aboard. The men provisioned the ship with stalks of green bananas and other fruits, and caught several sea turtles which were stowed live in the hold. We were ready for sea. All we lacked was the treasure.

Late that afternoon I was down in the foc'sle with Jibboom

when I heard a general outcry above. I hurried up the ladder and saw that we were setting sail. It gave me a start. The captain shouted orders fore and aft. Canvas unfurled and caught the breeze. We were leaving the cove.

"Oliver! Lend a hand at the capstan!"

I put my weight against a capstan bar, not knowing what to make of this sudden departure. Hajji leaned against a whipstaff opposite me and round and round we went, several of us, winding the chain as if on a great spool until the anchor was catted. Then Hajji gave me a threatening scowl and walked away.

We were standing out to sea when Captain Scratch called me to the poop deck. My only thought was of Jack o' Lantern watching from the jungle and seeing us sail away.

"Sir?"

The captain's broad back was toward me, but now he turned. I was astonished to find a smile on his face. "He's peeping at us, me lad! Aye, his deadlights is set this way."

He began to laugh, a kind of creaking sound like a door opening at night, and my heart began to thump. Did he know Jack o' Lantern was on the island? Was this some devilish joke?

"Peeping at us, sir?" I said, trying to keep my wits about me.

"Aye, he's a foxy spirit, is Gentleman Jack! He's seen us in the cove. Ain't we made enough noise to raise the dead? On his guard he's been, matey, and careful not to run up his colors. It's no wonder ye ain't clapped eyes on him. But seize me soul if I can't match tricks with him."

He was no wiser about Jack o' Lantern than before, but there was little comfort in it. I gazed past the taffrail at the island receding behind us—with Jack o' Lantern left ashore. "Tricks, sir?" I said, almost too anxiously.

Captain Scratch peered down at me and took a grip on his beard. "Aye."

"We'll be coming back?"

"You're game for another go at him, are ye?"

"Yes, sir."

"Stout lad," he murmured with satisfaction. "Hark, now— that peeping ghost sees us cruising off, doesn't he? Well, we'll come cruising back in the dark of night and catch him unawares!"

When the dark of night came, the captain ordered the ship about. There wasn't a scrap of moon in the sky and word was passed to douse all lights.

It was a couple of hours before we hove to and silently dropped anchor. I wondered what Jack o' Lantern had made of our disappearance and worried some that we might now catch him by surprise. I was tempted to show a light, a warning, but it would alert Gentleman Jack as well. The thought had hardly entered my mind when the captain ordered me into the longboat together with Cannibal and Hajji and John Ringrose. As we hung in the davits the pirates tied rags about the oars to silence them in the water. A pannikin of hog fat was handed up and we rubbed our faces and necks and arms to a high gloss.

Finally Captain Scratch climbed in after us. He carried his lantern with him, for the night darkness weighed heavily on him, but he didn't light it. "Lower away, mates!" he whispered hoarsely.

The boat hit the water, and I took a firm grip on one of the oars. Captain Scratch wrapped an arm around the tiller and urged us on in whispers. We rowed. Salt spray fell along my back like a heavy dew. We worked our way around the dark bulk of the headland. The surf cracked and lit up the cove with rushing foam.

The muffled oars made only the faintest lapping sounds in the sea. I bent my back with the others, and vowed that if there was a ghost above ground tonight, I'd see him. But, by thunder, I'd keep my wits. I'd ground-mark the spot for Jack o' Lantern to find, and send these buccaneers off in the wrong direction.

We rode the breakers into the shallows, leaped out and dragged the boat onto the beach. Night heat lay thick and heavy over the island and above us the star-shot sky gave off a sparkling glow.

"Not a sound, now, mates," Captain Scratch warned.

"Aye."

Noiselessly the pirates dug spades and shovels out of the longboat and shouldered them like muskets. The captain gave me a tap. "Lead on, me young sailorman. Skin your eyes for that cloudy gent, hear? Lay on, boy."

I looked about me, seeing nothing but the dark prickly shapes of the trees. Was the specter out there somewhere pacing the old treasure spot? I took a hopeful breath and we moved single file into the jungle.

I kept my eyes skinned. I was alert to every sound. We traveled as silently as fish through the sea. Hours passed. We crept. We paused. We crawled. Sweat ran down our backs in the furnace heat, and Captain Scratch's patience began to ebb. Toward midnight the moon rose, casting a pale light over the broad jungle leaves. And then we stopped for a parley.

"Don't ye see him?" the captain demanded.

"No, sir," I muttered.

"Where are your eyes, boy!"

We moved on and I peered everywhere. I kept one eye cocked for the ghost, the other for Jack o' Lantern—and both for a sweet, juicy genipa, for which my mouth watered. But I spied out neither one nor the other.

Again we stopped to parley, and now the captain's temper was soaring. "Don't ye see him!"

"No, sir."

"Blast your eyes!"

"Maybe there *is* no ghost," I answered, feeling temperish myself, and dog tired.

"No ghost! Are ye mad?"

"Maybe Gentleman Jack rests in his grave—rests easy. You told me yourself you avenged him on the spot. If he was ghosting around, I reckon I'd see him."

"Never mind what I said!" Captain Scratch growled, forgetting to keep his voice down. "I say there's a ghost about—that's what I say! Guarding the treasure, he is!"

"*Inshallah!*" came a hiss from Hajji. "May it please Allah, I see through this game the boy is playing on us."

"What's that?" the captain snapped.

"He throws dust in our eyes."

"What?"

Hajji grinned under the tattered rag of a turban wound around his head. "Do we know he hasn't already *seen* the ghostly one, eh captain? He'll be grown soon enough and can come back to the island—aye, and scoop up our golden booty for himself!"

"Hackle his bones!" Captain Scratch roared, grabbing me by

84 »

the ear. "Is that your foul scheme! Do ye think ye can out-sly me, ye mewling little fox!"

He gave my ear a twist and I cried out, "No, sir! I haven't seen Gentleman Jack! Not a glimpse!"

"You lie!" Hajji spat.

"We'll snatch the truth out of ye!" Captain Scratch said, almost lifting me off the ground by the ear.

"Hajji! Give him a taste of the Red Sea torture."

"The bastinado, Captain?"

"Aye." And he pitched me into Hajji's hands. "That'll learn him not to mince the truth with Harry Scratch!"

I didn't know what the Red Sea torture was, but I knew I wanted no part of it. I made a lurch to pull free, and thanks to the hog fat on my arms I slipped out of Hajji's grasp. But almost in the same instant Cannibal clapped hold of me and turned me upside down. By then my heart was banging away something fearful.

"Now, shipmates," I heard John Ringrose say in a soothing voice. "Don't let us be hasty with the bastinado. He's just a lad, Capting."

"Silence, ye overgrown cabin boy! Get on with it, Hajji."

While Cannibal held me upside down a jungle vine was tied around my ankles, my shoes were cast off, and the next thing I knew I was strung up from the limb of a tree—feet up and head down.

I was furious and I was scared. *"I haven't spied the ghost!"* I shouted. The blood was rushing to my head. *"That's the truth!"*

"Begin!" Captain Scratch commanded.

The Red Sea pirate began. He had armed himself with a hard stick and began to drum on the bare soles of my feet.

It hurt, but not overly much at first.

"Speak up, boy!" said Captain Scratch. "Don't tell me there's no ghost! Did ye get a flash of him, eh?"

"No, sir!"

"Are ye trying to frump me, boy? Me, that's treated ye as fair and honest as if ye were me own flesh and blood."

"Fair and honest!" I grimaced, dingling and dangling from the tree limb. Hajji kept stinging the soles of my feet and I jerked about like a fish on a line.

"Answer me, boy! The truth out of ye!"

"I'm telling you the truth!" I cried. "I haven't seen the ghost!"

"Don't lie to me, ye scurvy whelp!"

The stick rained down. The bottoms of my feet were now growing so hot and tender that each touch of the stick shot fire down my legs. I shut my eyes and grit my teeth, and still Hajji kept drumming away.

"Well, boy!"

I refused to answer. I was afraid now I would begin to cry if I opened my mouth. I could feel the hot sweat rolling along my legs and down my arms and off the hanging tips of my fingers.

"Answer me, boy!"

"Cut him down," John Ringrose said, in a quiet, begging voice.

"Aye—when we bastinado the truth out of him!"

"Capting, it's the truth he's trying to tell ye."

"Hold your tongue, John! Unless ye want your own feet keeled up."

Hajji kept thrashing away until I thought one more lam of the stick would shatter my feet like glass. I opened my eyes and looked around at the upside-down figure of Captain Scratch. If it was a lie he wanted—tarnation, I'd give it to him! I'd say I'd seen the ghost and be done with it!

But before I could spit out the words they caught in my throat. Hanging topsy-turvy, I spied a glow in the bushes. A vaporish shape! It was him! I all but cried out, but clamped my teeth hard—long enough to gather my feverish wits. And then I swung an arm around to point in the opposite direction.

"I see him!" I cried. "He's there now! The ghost, sir! *It's Gentleman Jack!*"

CHAPTER 11

*In which things happen
one after the other—most of
them fast and furious*

"AFTER HIM! After him, lad!" Captain Scratch rumbled, charging forward and forgetting for the moment that I was left dangling from the tree. I tried to take another fix on the ghost, but he had tacked out of sight.

There was now the wildest confusion among us. In their haste to cut me down, John Ringrose and Hajji butted heads. The Red Sea sailor went bowling backwards with such force that he disappeared into the bushes and failed to get up again. Ringrose let out a laugh and I suspected he had rapped skulls on purpose. I wasn't sure if he had taken a disliking to Hajji or a liking to me.

"Blast ye for fools!" Captain Scratch crackled. He drew his cutlass and whacked through the vine. I hit the ground on my hands and tumbled over. "Quick, lad! The ghost! The ghost! Keep your deadlights on him!"

Loosening the vine from around my ankles, again I tried to spy out Gentleman Jack. He was gone. We were making such a racket it wouldn't surprise me if he had seeped back into his grave.

Quickly, I ground-marked the spot. I found my jackknife, which had slipped out of my pocket, opened the blade and stabbed it into the earth. I was careful to set the handle in the direction I had seen Gentleman Jack appear.

"After him, boy!" Captain Scratch commanded in a hushed voice. "Don't lose him!"

I tried to get to my feet and collapsed to my knees. "I can't walk," I whispered.

"What's that?"

"My feet, sir."

Captain Scratch gave a furious gasp. "The devil seize that Red Sea imbecile! I'll croak him with me own hands!" And then he stuck his nose in my face, and remembered to lower his voice. "Is the gentleman still out there, Oliver lad? Do ye see him?"

"He's gone," I said.

"Hackle his bones! Gone?"

"Yes, sir."

"But ye saw him standing off this way, did ye?"

"More or less."

"More or less, say ye?"

"I was upside down at the time," I reminded him in a spleenish tone.

"Well, was he *this* way or *that,* boy!"

"More *that* than *this,* I think," said I. The bottoms of my feet felt as if wasps were swarming on them, stinging away. I tried to pull on my shoes but couldn't get my swollen feet into them. Captain Scratch bristled at the delay. The Red Sea torture now pained him as much as it did me. Because of it we would lose the ghost for sure.

Finally, John Ringrose hoisted me onto his back. "Rest easy, sonny," he whispered. "Yer feet'll be good as new in no time, but that swine Hajji—he'll be nursin' his noggin for a week." And then he chuckled softly.

"Belay that jabber!" Captain Scratch said. "Forward, forward! He may still be lurking about!"

For half an hour we went creeping around in small circles with the captain sniffing the air for brimstone. We raised nothing but the chirp of crickets, and insects buzzing and whining through the heat like birdshot. Finally Captain Scratch called a halt.

"About here, was he?"

"There," I said, paying no particular attention where I pointed. By thunder, I'd let him stew and simmer.

He took a step deeper into the jungle. "Here, say ye?"

"A shade more *here* than there," I answered. "But a mite more *there* than here."

He made a half-step forward. "Is this the spot, boy?"

"About."

"Aye. Gentleman Jack must have popped up out of the ground to watch the bastinado. All aglow was he?"

"Steaming like a tea kettle," I said, laying it on thicker than necessary.

"Decked out in his scarlet coat, was he?"

I didn't remember the coat at all, but that didn't stop me. "Red as fire, sir. With the sleeve missing."

"Aye! That was him for sure." He lit the lantern and hung it from the limb of a tree. "We'll start digging here."

During the long dark hours of morning the pirates spaded up the earth. I slept. I slept under a banana tree and when the sun woke me the buccaneers were still at their shovels. The ragged pit had grown as broad as a cellar.

I had no great interest in it. Captain Scratch would find no treasure in this spot. I listened to the morning talk of birds and ate my fill of bananas. I crawled to a trickle of water among the rocks and soothed my feet as best I could. They were as scarlet as Gentleman Jack's coat and looked twice the size of my shoes.

"Dig away, me hearties," Captain Scratch sang out from time to time. "Bend your backbones, me lads. We can't be far off the spot now."

Men were fetched off the *Bloody Hand* and the digging went on throughout the day. Dirt flew. I was sorry to see John Ringrose going at it full chisel and to no use, but I didn't mind seeing Hajji at hard labor, wincing as if there was a woodpecker knocking away inside his skull. The excavation lengthened and broadened. I had a feeling Jack o' Lantern was watching the goings on, but he was careful to keep out of sight.

"Look sharp for the skeleton, mates. That'll be Gentleman Jack—may his timbers rest in peace. The gold boxes you'll find just below him."

But as the day wore on hopes began to lag. The pit was now a vast hollow reaching around the trees, and Captain Scratch took to pacing and pulling at his wild red beard and mumbling to himself. The sun was lowering when he cocked an eye at the diggings and gave a cantankerous snort.

"Look at ye! Blast ye for a pack of sea apes, what do ye think you're about, mates?"

Ezra Fly paused to rest an arm on the handle of his shovel and looked the captain square in the eye. "Digging for treasure," he said, "according to your orders."

"Treasure! Gold! Can't ye see there's nothing under your feet but seashells and sand? Belay them shovels, boys. We've missed the spot. Aye, we've missed it." He found me among the rocks nearby and stared down at me. "Ye saw him, did ye?"

"Yes, sir."

"Through these trees, was he?"

"Yes and no, sir."

"Confound your confounded answers, boy!"

"One tree looks like the next when you're hanging by the heels," said I. "And it was mortal dark." He could bluster all he wanted, but he wasn't going to get the bettermost of me. *He* was hanging by the heels now. He could dig all the way to China and he wouldn't find the treasure in this spot. Once we returned to the ship, Jack o' Lantern would find my knife stuck in the ground and that would give him a true fix on Gentleman Jack.

"Aye, but ye saw him with your own eyes, lad—steaming up in his scarlet coat, like ye told me."

"Yes, sir." And once Jack o' Lantern hauled up those boxes of plunder he was going to clap the villain out of Captain Scratch. That would be a sight to see.

He shut one eye thoughtfully. "That's the proof. Aye, you've got the ghosting power—and by the shrouds, if you've seen him once, you'll see him once again!" He began to chuckle. "Why, he was roving about in the trees to mislead us, lad.

That's as clear as glass. It wouldn't catch me by surprise if that treasure is stowed clear the other side of the island."

Suddenly there came a shout from below in the diggings. "Strike me ugly!" John Ringrose cried out. He began to flap about like a scrawny bird trying to fly. "I hit it, Capting! Aye! There's a chest down here!"

The pirates closed in on the spot like flies. Captain Scratch leaped away from me and almost tripped over his cutlass. I crawled closer and watched as best I could.

"Bless the mark!" Captain Scratch laughed. "That's it, boys!"

Soon the dirt was flying again. In a burst of impatience Captain Scratch grabbed a spade away from one of the men and began going at the box himself. Moment by moment more of it came into view. My heart beat away now in a kind of icy dread. How could I have got my directions so muddled? We were lost now, Jack o' Lantern and I. Even topsy-turvy, I had put them onto the treasure and now Captain Scratch would have no further need of me. The future darkened with every spade of earth. I was as good as marooned.

But as I watched I wondered why the bones of Gentleman Jack hadn't turned up. Hadn't he been shot and fallen over the treasure as it was being buried—the way Captain Scratch described it?

Within minutes the box was hauled up, and so heavy with treasure was it that four men lent their arms to lift it. "Easy, lads," said Captain Scratch. "Back up, boys, and let's have a look at it. Seven years it's been. Aye, seven years."

"It's only a sea chest," said Ezra Fly.

"A sea chest!" Captain Scratch grimaced, wiping the sweat

out of his eyes. "Aye, a sea chest. I disremember that we buried a sea chest. And there was more. Three boxes in all."

Dirt flew again, but there was only the single iron-clad sea chest to be found. My hopes took a leap. This wasn't Gentleman Jack's treasure—it couldn't be. By thunder, we had stumbled over another buccaneer's plunder.

"And so much the better," Captain Scratch laughed. "Gold is gold, I say, and let's have a look at it."

In high and feverish spirits now the men began banging away at the heavy lock with shovels and spades, but the lock resisted. Finally Captain Scratch stepped in with his cutlass and gave the lock a whack, breaking off the end of the weapon. He cursed and ordered the box carried to the longboat. "We'll chisel it open aboard ship, mates. Aye, that's the ticket."

It was dusk before the chest was hauled on deck. The western sky glowed like a forge and cast a blood-red light over the buccaneers. Big Nose Ned went at the lock with hammer and chisel.

I tried to hobble about, but it would have been easier to walk over broken glass, or so it seemed to me. I sat against the heel of the mainmast with my feet thrust out in front of me.

At last there came a shout from the men around the sea chest. The lock had given way. "Step back," Captain Scratch said. "Not too close. Why, from the heft of it, boys, there's gold and jewels enough under that lid to blind ye at close quarters. Aye, it'll be like looking straight at the sun!"

Chuckling, his greedy eyes set, he threw back the lid. My own heart skipped a beat. Not a man moved. They gazed into the sea chest, and it was as if the sight of all those riches turned them to stone. I crawled forward on my hands and knees for a closer look and watched through Cannibal's long legs.

Peering into the box, Captain Scratch now gave an awful snort. "Gold! Jewels!" He dug into the chest with both hands. "The devil fetch him—what pirate's foul joke is this!" He raised black lumps the size of apples. "Cannonballs!" he roared. "Aye, cannonballs! We've been jigamareed, boys! There's treasure for ye! Let's see ye spend these iron doubloons in London Town!" He was hugely angry and flung the five-pounders at a flock of gulls milling and squawking to windward. The heavy balls shot through the air as trim as stones and sank—*kerslosh*! "Cannonballs!" he bellowed. He gave the chest a kick and went storming off to his cabin for the night.

John Ringrose hauled me up two buckets of sea water. I ate my supper with a foot soaking in each bucket. I wanted to let him know that I was privy to Jack o' Lantern's plan, but there always seemed to be somebody lingering about, and I kept my mouth shut.

Once darkness fell Captain Scratch sprang out of his cabin and demanded to know who had the dredgy watch. No one answered or volunteered, and Ringrose had the misfortune at that moment to be coming up the foc'sle hatch. The captain spied him and commanded him to take the watch.

"Aye, Capting," Ringrose answered, cheerfully enough, even though he had been without a wink of sleep all the night before. Soon he was making the rounds, swinging a lantern, on the lookout for wet footprints.

It being hot and airless below, I decided to spend the night on deck. Jibboom went prowling about for a while and then crouched along the ship's rail. His one eye shone on me like a yellow star. He seemed out of sorts with me for having gone ashore without him.

It had been a hard day for the buccaneers, with a grist of disappointments. One by one they went to their bunks, and round and round the decks went John Ringrose.

I watched the mast tops swaying back and forth through the stars, and thought about the ghost. As near as I could recollect what I had seen, he had heaved right up through the ground itself. That spook hadn't been adventuring about, as Captain Scratch believed. No, sir. I had set my jackknife directly on him. That's where the treasure was.

I kept falling asleep and the soles of my feet kept waking me up. The ship had grown silent. We swung on the anchor chain, the timbers creaking and sighing. I was tempted now to parley with John Ringrose and waited for him to come around. But he didn't show up.

I raised myself to my elbows and gazed about. There was Jibboom now asleep on the rail, and there was John Ringrose resting his long bones against the poopdeck ladder. He hung there like a puppet on strings, the lamp burning away at his feet.

What I saw next caused me to jump out of my skin. *I saw wet footprints!*

They made a glistening trail along the quarterdeck. My eyes shot along the tracks to a strange figure dripping in the shadows, a knife clamped between his teeth. John Ringrose was staring full at him—*didn't he see him?*

Now another figure climbing up from the sea leaped the rail and boarded us. The hair was stiff on my scalp. Of course Ringrose didn't see them—he couldn't. *But I could.* And I let out a yell.

"*Dredgies!*" I shouted, at the very top of my lungs. "*Dredgies! We're boarded by dredgies!*"

CHAPTER 12

The night of the dredgies, and how it ended

H ARDLY TWO seconds passed before a knife came hurtling through the air to silence me. It thudded in wood and hummed an inch from my ear. Until I heard myself shouting the alarm I wasn't overly convinced of dredgies. But there they were before my eyes, crawling up from the brine.

I stilled my tongue and rolled away from the knife. My cries jerked Ringrose awake—he had fallen asleep on his feet—and he picked up the alarm. *"Dredgies!"* he shouted and dove out of sight.

He had hardly uttered the word when Captain Scratch burst out of his cabin, with the end of a long sleeping cap dangling over one eye. Hearing the fearsome battle cry he turned white as a bone. *"Dredgies!"* he gasped, and leaping back he slammed the cabin door. Meanwhile, the crew came tumbling up through the foc'sle hatch, but hearing his alarm—they tumbled back down again.

Suddenly all was silence.

The sea made gentle lapping sounds along the hull and the ship groaned in its joints. Mr. Ringrose's lantern, left at the foot of the ladder, glowed and flickered. I crept under a tangle of rope. Jibboom was gone from the rail.

I counted four dredgies—and a fifth climbing up from the sea. He balanced himself on the rail, with the sea brine rolling off his arms and short legs. He was scaresome to see. Long yellow hair clung to his skull like sea grass, and great hanging moustaches dripped from his face. His eyes darted about, picking out his fellows in the shadows.

"Well, dash my wig!" he said, giving himself the highflown air of an English duke. I think he would have taken a dip of snuff if he had brought some with him out of the deep. And then his voice turned chirpy as a cricket. "What keeps you standing about for? Mongrels! Cowards! Waiting for some scurvy chap to slit your throats?"

"There's no fight in this crew," came the reply.

"Aye," whispered another. "The ship's spooked."

And another cried out, *"Dios!"* There's dredgies aboard, *compadre. Si*—I can see the wet tracks with my own eyes!"

"Spanish blockhead!" the little man exploded. "Those are your own footprints! Fight, you palpitating pigeons! Charge, you cowering geese! To the captain's quarters!"

So saying he jumped to deck. A piercing screech ripped through the night air. It was a cry I knew well. He had landed on Jibboom's tail.

I was by this time already grown duberous about this boarding party of dead men from the brine. Dredgies? A dredgy didn't have *weight* enough to step on a cat's tail! My moon-

struck fancies fled. Tarnation!—*these were common cutthroats!
And they had come to murder us in our sleep!*

The man with the hanging moustaches was picking himself
up off the deck. "Infernal cat!" he snapped. "Attack, I say. To
the captain's cabin!"

They leaped to it. I didn't linger on the spot. I slid around
the deck house, thinking to arouse the crew to our present dan-
ger, but when I reached the foc'sle hatch I found it locked tight.
I rapped with my fist, but raised no one. The men below must
have thought it was the dead men come to get them.

I gave it up and scurried aft along the deck like a crab. The
invaders were now charging the captain's cabin. I stopped behind the chest of cannonballs and saw them batter at the door
with their shoulders. The lock burst and they rushed into the
dark cabin, lickety-cut, yelling like banshees. Clearly, the captain
had doused his night lantern in order to hide himself away.

And then, inches from my nose, the lid of the old sea chest
began to rise on its rusty, creaking hinges. My breath caught.
Something was rising out of the chest—slowly, slowly. I was
too awestruck to move. A long, bony hand was lifting the lid as
if it were a coffin. I gaped. I gasped.

And I found myself staring into the startled face of John
Ringrose.

"You!" I gulped.

"You!" he gulped, for I had scared him in his hiding place as
much as he did me. How he had folded himself up in there with
the cannonballs was a marvel.

"Quick, sir!" I said. "They're not dredgies—they're cutthroats!"

"Nay, sonny," he twitched, lowering the lid again.

"See for yourself!"

By now the rogues had burst back on deck, flinging Captain Scratch along with them. In the tussle the sleeping cap had got pulled all the way down over his face.

"Strike me ugly!" said Ringrose, peeping at them. "Why, they're—they're merely murderers!"

"Spaniards, I think!"

He was aghast. "Spaniards!"

"One of them, at least. They plan to take the ship from us!"

"Spaniards." The word seemed to bring him to life like a battle cry. I had never seen him move so fast. He heaved himself out of the chest and found that he had lost the pistol out of his belt. He wasted no time on that but immediately slipped off his long canvas breeches.

Believing himself to be in the grip of dredgies, Captain Scratch was putting up no fight at all. He let himself be moved along like a blind man, babbling through the sleeping cap, and all a-quiver. "Ye found me, shipmates," he said, muffle-voiced. "Is it thee, Dick? Is it thee, Ben? Aye, I knew you'd come for me. And thee, Timothy. I been expecting ye in the night, shipmates. Come to punish me, have ye? Aye, I deserve it. And then some, I do. Oh, I regret what I done, boys, making ye walk the plank the way I did—me very own shipmates."

"Dash my wig!" said the chief of the rogues. "What's this sniveling fool bleating about? String him up, my bullies. From the yardarm! That'll show the crew what brand of insolence we're about!"

What Ringrose was up to I couldn't make out. He had tied a knot in the bottom of one trouser leg, and now he was tying a knot in the other.

"But don't ye see, shipmates, I had to do it," Captain Scratch babbled on. "Ye knew me secret, each of ye. Aye, ye were all standing there when we was sinking the treasure. And ye saw that terrible awful thing I done, putting a bullet in our captain's stout heart. Him, that was the best of us all. Aye, and elected meself captain in his place."

I stared. So that was how it had happened! It was Captain Scratch himself who had done in Gentleman Jack. And of course he didn't lie easy in his grave. He hadn't been avenged at all! He couldn't rest—not with Captain Scratch unpunished. By thunder, he deserved to be strung up from the yardarm!

But if he received his punishment at the hands of these bloodthirsty rovers, if Gentleman Jack were avenged now—tarnation!—the island ghost would be laid. If I were off the mark with my jackknife, there would be no rising vapors, no spook, to fix the treasure spot again. It would be lost forever.

By the time these thoughts had gone flying through my head, Mr. Ringrose had dropped a cannonball into each leg of his breeches. The knots at the bottoms kept the iron from falling through. He was so busy at his task that he seemed to pay no attention to Captain Scratch's confession.

But now he jumped up and began swinging the weighted trousers around his head. He let fly. The canvas breeches flashed aft and the long legs wrapped themselves like tentacles around the party of cutthroats.

"Spaniards! Spaniards, Capting!" Ringrose shouted. "It's Spaniards has got ye!"

The cry awoke Captain Scratch from the grip of his dredgy madness. He was wrapped together with his captors like a bunch of carrots, but now he gave a roaring heave and snatched the nightcap off his head.

"Spaniards!"

They broke out of the tangle of John Ringrose's breeches, and knives flashed. Captain Scratch picked up one of the wasters bodily and pitched him into the others. At the same time, Ringrose began skimming cannonballs along deck as if he were playing at duckpins. I jumped to it myself.

The cutthroats were now kept as busy as bees in a tar barrel. They began hopping about as if the deck was on fire. Captain Scratch hurled one of the men over the side, and then another. A third climbed out on the ratlines, but Ringrose heaved such a charge of cannonballs his way that he soon fell into the sea. The fourth man jumped over the side on his own advice.

But there was more fight in their leader than all his fellows combined. Captain Scratch, deep in the shadows, couldn't lay hands on him. The little man leaped about like a flea, a knife between his teeth and another in his hand. Captain Scratch lunged like an enraged bull and clasped thin air. Finally, he caught the rogue by the foot as he tried to get into the riggings. Then, the last of the cannonballs, which I myself had fired along deck, tripped Captain Scratch. In the next second the little man was on top of him, knife in the air, their two heads now in the glow of the dredgy lantern left on deck.

"Harry Scratch!" the little man gasped, the knife frozen in midair.

In that same instant Captain Scratch recognized the man he was fighting. "The devil fetch me!" he roared. "It's Billy Bombay!"

CHAPTER 13

*In which we are
again thirteen*

BILLY BOMBAY! I gazed with a kind of wonder at the crickety little man who, like myself, had the power to spy out ghosts. Fighting to the death a moment before, the two buccaneers now burst into huge gales of laughter.

"Dash my wig!" said one.

"Seize me soul!" said the other.

"I ain't laid eyes on you since we cruised the Campeachy coast."

"Aye—ten years, if it's been a day, Billy. But I combed the seas for ye, I did, and—ha!—now it's yourself has found me."

"Loo! Another second and I'd have slit your throat!"

"Bilge!" said Captain Scratch, grinning through his wild beard. "Another *half*-second and I'd have wrung your neck."

"Tut-tut!"

"Blast ye for a cunning little peacock—we took ye for Spaniards!"

Suddenly reminded of his comrades, Billy Bombay snatched up the lantern and held it over the rail. "Helloo-o-o, ship-mates!" he called. "Any lads afloat down there? Avast!"

There came no answering call from the water.

Captain Scratch hurled a command along deck. "Lower the boat! Damnation! Where's the pack of cowards that man this ship?"

"It's too late for the boat," sighed Billy Bombay, cupping an ear to the night. "Sunk like stones, I fancy. Not a one of them can swim a stroke any more than I can. May their sweet souls rest in peace—do you have a snort of grog aboard, Harry?"

"Cabin boy!" snapped Captain Scratch. "You, John—rum for our guest."

"Aye, Capting," said Ringrose. "I could use a nip myself."

"Lord save me, John, since when do ye drink with *gentlemen*? And what are ye standing about for in your scrawny legs? Do ye think you're a stork? Where are your breeches?"

"Why, I saved yer life with 'em, Capting."

"Bilge, and more bilge! Fetch the grog, ye witless scarecrow!"

The cannonballs had mostly rolled to the scuppers and dropped one by one into the sea. Mr. Ringrose gathered up his canvas trousers and up-ended them. A five-pounder tumbled out of each leg, clattered to deck and joined the others in the deep.

"Dash my wig! So it's *Captain* Scratch, is it now?" grinned Billy Bombay. "Loo! You was just a foc'sle hand when we shipped together last."

"Aye, Billy. I've come up in the world. A gentleman I am these days—why, I can almost write me own name. How did ye get here? Is your ship standing off in the dark there?"

"Ship?" the little man scowled, and began twirling out his

long moustache. He then explained that he and his comrades, including a renegade Spaniard, had escaped captivity on the island of Hispaniola. They had secretly carved a wherry-boat out of a fallen cedar log and set their course for this very island. They had been six days at sea. At dusk they had sighted not only the island but also a ship at anchor. They determined to take us. Fearing that we might spy their canoe, Billy Bombay had ordered his men over the side and turned the boat keel up. They had then pushed it along like a floating log and come slowly skulking toward us in the night. They had waited alongside until the ship fell silent. When Billy Bombay judged that our crew was asleep, he gave the order to board and fight. But first he had cut a hole in the wherry-boat, swamped and sunk it—to spur his men on. There would be no turning back. They must do or die.

"But, loo! they thought the ship was spooked with dredgies and began jumping about at their own shadows."

"Dredgies," Captain Scratch scoffed, as if he had never heard anything so monstrous foolish. "Dredgies on *my* ship? Me, that never harmed a seafaring soul?"

Billy Bombay screwed up one eye and laughed. "You? Why, you yourself was cowering under your bunk like a mouse when we broke in. We wouldn't have found you at all if we hadn't heard your teeth chattering."

"Cowering! Why, why—I was nightmarish! Me solemn oath upon the Holy Evangelists, if I wasn't. Aye, with fever! Oh, when the chills come on ye—why, a man can't keep his teeth from clacking away. I tell ye, the fever's bad in these waters, Billy."

"And what was you yammering about—men walking the plank, and murder?"

"Sea yarns! It was that pestiferous fever talking in me sleep, I tell ye. But when I awoke and found ye trying to string me up from the yards—that made me enormous mad, Billy. Why, it's a miracle you're standing here alive!"

"Tut-tut."

"Did I hear ye say ye set your course for this island?"

"This very one."

Captain Scratch lowered a crafty eyebrow. "Why, there's nothing here, man. Nothing but sea turtles and boars and banana trees."

"And treasure," Billy Bombay muttered airily, his moustache now drawn out as long and sharp as hat pins.

Captain Scratch's face clouded with suspicion. I could guess what he was thinking. Did Billy Bombay already know about the ghost of Gentleman Jack? Was that why he had come—to dig up those boxes of plunder for himself? "Treasure, did ye say!"

"Enough for us both. I'll share out with you, Harry, since you've got a ship under your feet. I'll want safe passage to Tortuga."

Captain Scratch filled up like a frog and I thought he'd explode. "*You'll* share out with *me*, ye beggar! You'll be lucky if I don't cut ye up for fish bait! I don't need your blasted eyes to spy me the ghost. I've got a pair of ghosting eyes aboard."

"Ghost? What ghost?"

Captain Scratch stilled his tongue. And then his gaze narrowed curiously. "Treasure? What treasure?"

"Spanish plunder. I buried it myself in an old sea chest and it's been waiting for me all these years."

"A *sea chest*, did ye say?"

"Aye."

By this time John Ringrose had come up from below with rum bottles cradled in his arms, but Captain Scratch shoved him aside. He picked up the lantern and led Billy Bombay forward to the sea chest that lay open and empty on deck.

"Is this the box?" demanded Captain Scratch.

Billy Bombay went over the chest with his hands and then peered up at Captain Scratch. "So you found it, did you?"

Captain Scratch burst out laughing. "Have the Spaniards addled your wits, Billy? There was nothing in that box but cannonballs!"

"Five-pounders, they was," John Ringrose grinned. "Aye, that's what we skittered along deck to keep ye dancin', Oliver here and meself."

"Cannonballs!" Billy Bombay cried, and began jumping about in a mortal rage. "Five-pounders! Nitwits! Blockheads! Don't you know black tarnish from iron? They was Spanish silver! Silver, I tell you. Melted down and cast in five-pounder molds to fool thieves! A fortune in silver, it was—and you pitched it over the side!"

Captain Scratch rolled his eyes and gave out an awful sigh. He fell into such a temper that I thought he would hurl the both of us into the sea. We were anchored in deep water and there was no hope of raising the silver horde. "Ringrose! Imbecile!" he roared, forgetting that he himself had heaved the first two cannonballs at seagulls. "See what you've done! Out of me sight, before I forget I'm a gentleman!"

He was even forgetting that we had helped save his life, but John Ringrose decided he was in no temper to be reminded of it. "Aye, Capting," he said. "I'll move meself ashore, we now being thirteen aboard ship again."

"Begone!"

"I'll go too," I said. "I'm as much at fault as Mr. Ringrose."

"Silence! You'll stay by me side where ye belong!" He narrowed one eye and began stroking his beard. "Aye, between yourself and Billy Bombay—we'll close in on the vaporous gent like crossfire!"

Ringrose was glad enough to duck out of sight. He went below to fetch his sea chest. Captain Scratch and Billy Bombay made a search of the decks, but not a single cannonball could be found. They gathered up the bottles of rum and retired to the captain's quarters, grumbling and swearing, to drown their disappointments.

Jibboom came twining around me, flicking his sore tail, and raising his back for me to scratch. I think we were making each other homesick. We talked to each other in low voices and then John Ringrose appeared through the foc'sle hatch with a sea chest on his back. He lowered a skiff and dropped the jack ladder over the side. My feet were next to useless, but I got myself to the rail.

"Mr. Ringrose," I said quietly.

"Aye, sonny." He had a rope around his sea chest and began to lower it to the rowboat.

"I've joined up with Jack o' Lantern."

"What?"

"I know he's ashore."

"Well—strike me ugly!"

"I *did* see Gentleman Jack," I whispered. "Only not where I said he was. Tell Jack o' Lantern I set my jackknife in the ground to mark the exact direction. Tell him to walk about twenty paces forward of it. That's where the treasure is."

His head jerked toward me. The rope burned through his

hands and the sea chest banged into the skiff. His jaw fell like a trapdoor. I had never seen him with such a look of surprisal on his face. Slowly he dug through his pockets and handed me what, for an instant, I took to be a dark twig. "I thought you'd dropped it," he groaned. "I was meanin' to give it back to ye."

It was my jackknife.

CHAPTER 14

In which things come to
light, in more ways
than one

FOR TWO days and nights Captain Scratch hardly stirred from his cabin except to shout for more rum. The Red Sea torture wore off my feet and the next night I was tramping around the island again, in company with Billy Bombay. Captain Scratch had such a tempest howling through his head that he remained aboard. He waved us off in the longboat and gave us to understand that the one who first spied Gentleman Jack would share in the treasure. "Aye," he snorted. "And the other—why, the other of ye we'll fling to the fishes!"

"Fair enough," answered Billy Bombay, who was bleary-eyed and peaky-looking himself. He regarded me with a twistical smile. "One of us is a goner."

"Yes, sir," I muttered.

"So you was midnight born like myself. How many ghosts have you seen?"

"One—so far," I said.

"Loo! I've seen 'em leaping about as common as fleas. I can spot 'em with one eye shut. You're out-matched, boy. I do hate to tell you that."

I didn't answer. He was talking to keep his courage up, I told myself. He had dandified his yellow hair and kept testing the points of his moustache, but the grog had left his eyes as red as coals. He wasn't at all certain he'd be the first to fetch up the ghost and was feeling peskily worried about it. There was no mistake—we were deadly enemies.

I wished suddenly I had brought Jibboom along. If worst came to worst I wouldn't return to the ship.

Once ashore, Billy Bombay told the other men along with us to remain in the cove. "I don't want a pack of noisy swabs dogging us. You've got to slip up on a ghost, quiet-like."

After that the two of us put off into the trees. I decided I would give Billy Bombay the slip before he throttled me in the dark. By thunder, that was why he didn't want the other men along. He wouldn't take the chance of my spying the ghost first. There was foul play up his sleeve. He meant to dispatch me for sure.

I glanced about for John Ringrose. There was no sign of him except for the skiff left high and dry on the beach.

"This way, boy," Billy Bombay said.

I backed away. He kept stalking forward and then he must have turned to pounce and do me in. But I wasn't there. Through the darkness I could hear him fizz and sizzle. "Dash my wig! Dash my wig!"

I streaked it for the hollow of the island where the chest of silver cannonballs had been dug up. I had seen Gentleman Jack shying about the spot and that was the place for me to snug myself. I hid in a bush—and something jumped out.

My heart bounced a mile. It was like a log come to life. It went crashing through the leaves—dark and snorting. And then it was gone and I knew what it was. I had tried to share a bush with a wild boar. I took a gulp of air and when I stopped shaking I climbed a tree. I felt safer up there. And I could see all around. I'd wait for Gentleman Jack.

I kept hoping that John Ringrose or Jack o' Lantern might turn up. They ought to be rooting around for the treasure nearby, knowing I had already caught a glimpse of the ghost in the neighborhood. But a couple of hours passed and nothing stirred below me except an occasional firefly streaking through the blackness like a spark. I began to worry that something had happened to them.

And then, so sudden that I had to hang on to keep from falling out of the tree—I spied Gentleman Jack!

My eyes must almost have jumped out of my head. He was a scaresome thing, all aglow in a coat as red as blood and a floppy hat on his head, with a long plume on it. He was loping away through the jungle like a ball of fire and almost before I could think what to do I was skinning down the tree. The crickets were clacking away like skeletons dancing. There was Gentleman Jack before my very eyes, and I meant to hang on to his glowing coattails. He'd lead me to the treasure spot itself!

He didn't go far. He hid behind a tree. Then he leaped to a slab of rock as if he didn't care who saw him, and began to pace. I crept closer, in a cold sweat, and spread a tangle of leaves to watch him. Suddenly he raised one arm and pointed with a long finger.

"Hark ye!" he said, in a deep, wrathy voice. "Begone, varlet!"

My knees turned as limsy as molasses. He was almost pointing at me—but not precisely. There was someone in the cluster of banana trees to my right. Billy Bombay? Jack o' Lantern? John Ringrose? If it hadn't been for the crickets, my own rattling teeth would have given me away.

"Begone, I say!" he snorted, his finger outstretched like a twig. The plume in his hat sparkled like diamonds. The ghostly glow about him flickered as if the merest breeze would snuff him out like a candle.

"Loo!" came an awful gasp from the banana trees. And then, as if prodded by a bolt of lightning, Billy Bombay came whapping over the jungle bushes and ran so close by me that I could see him. He was in a terrible state of amazement, with his mouth wide open and not a sound coming out. It seemed hardly an instant before he was gone.

I held my ground. I'd be the one to see where it was that Gentleman Jack seeped back into his grave. But he didn't move, except to slowly lower his arm. And then he cupped an ear as if he could hear my teeth and seemed to stare straight at me. My heart absolutely stopped.

And then he began to laugh—a quick, cackling laugh. "Avast, Oliver. Out with ye, sonny." He whipped off his hat and gave me a bow.

It was John Ringrose.

Hardly a moment passed before Jack o' Lantern appeared, in a perfect fit of laughter. "Did ye see Billy run? Why, ye'd think he never saw a ghost before!"

Mr. Ringrose was still aglow and I couldn't get my bones to stop shaking, not for a couple of minutes. He began to scratch and pull open the coat. "The blighters has crawled down me neck," he complained.

"Glowworms," Jack o' Lantern said to me. "The fireflies lay 'em. John and me has been busy collecting 'em from the underside of leaves. Aye, John is as wormy as an apple!"

Mr. Ringrose stripped off the red coat and when he threw it to the ground it lit up like fire. "Help me get 'em off me!" he cried, shivering around as if he had the chills. "The blighters is down me back!"

Worm by worm the ghostly glow was plucked off him, but I was sunk in my own troubles. Billy Bombay would swear to Captain Scratch that he had seen the ghost, and they'd lose no time ridding themselves of me.

"So that's the ticket is it," Jack o' Lantern said, when I explained matters to him. "But the laugh is up yer sleeve, lad. Don't ye see, when John here told me that Billy Bombay had turned up, we couldn't let him beat us to Gentleman Jack, could we? So we fixed up this little welcome for him with some duds out of John's sea chest—him hoping to rise to the quality of admiral at least, from the look of them. Can ye see Captain Scratch's face when Billy leads him back to solid rock? Why, he'll split Billy Bombay in two on the spot!"

"But I *saw* Gentleman Jack," I said. "Not far from where the cannonballs were buried."

"Nay, bucko. That was a handful of these worms ye saw—*cochinillas,* as the Spaniards call 'em. I couldn't let Hajji keep banging away at yer feet that night, could I? I fancied ye'd yell out if ye saw something light up. It took me a while to pluck off a handful of the buggers, they not being overly plentiful on this island—or else ye wouldn't have been kept hanging by yer ankles so long. Anyway, I hid back and tossed the bugs in the air for ye. They do brighten up when ye give 'em a fright that way. Well now, bucko, you'll stay here with us and we'll wait for Captain Scratch to come calling on that rock!"

But Captain Scratch didn't turn up. The night passed and it was an hour after dawn before we spied the longboat heading back into the cove. Captain Scratch and Cannibal stepped ashore. Billy Bombay was nowhere among them.

"Oliver!" Captain Scratch called. "Where be ye, lad?"

I exchanged glances with Jack o' Lantern and Mr. Ringrose, and kept mum.

"Oliver! Ye didn't take me serious, did ye? Ye don't think I meant what I said—feeding ye to the fishes! Why, it was only a joke, boy. Are ye hiding from me? Me, that means to do the best by ye? Is it Billy Bombay that worries ye? Lord save me, he ain't any good to us. Lost his power of speech, he has. Walking around like a coconut fell on his skull. Where are ye, boy!"

He took another few steps along the beach and when I didn't answer, he gave a signal to Cannibal. My heart skipped a beat, for I had a foreboding the moment I saw that Fiji savage reach into the longboat and come up with a canvas bag.

"Boy, I'll give ye *sixty* seconds to step forward! That's your cat in the bag, and if ye want him before I wrings his neck, you'll have to come get him!"

CHAPTER 15

Being full of the most
interesting things imaginable

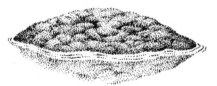

THE SIGHT of that red-bearded villain made me as mad as all wrath. Jack o' Lantern had to hold me down.

"Easy, bucko."

"The capting is a tricksy one, ain't he?" John Ringrose said, peering out through the bushes.

"We'll show him a trick or two," Jack o' Lantern muttered. "But we'll need the treasure to do it."

"*Seven!*" shouted Captain Scratch from the beach, counting off the seconds. He pulled Jibboom out of the canvas bag and held him up by the scruff of the neck. "*Eight! Nine! Ten!*" Jibboom pawed the air, but couldn't free himself from the captain's huge hand. "*Eleven! Twelve!*"

"Let loose of me!" I spit. "I'm going down there!"

"Of course ye are," Jack o' Lantern whispered. "But give us a moment to cogitate matters. And cool yer head. It won't do no good to go down there all a-simmer." He eased up on me. "John, I'd say we called Billy Bombay's bluff. I don't think he ever saw a ghost in his life until last night—aye, and it sent his wits flying like bats. He was just boast and bombast, trying to cut a splurge—making himself important, ye know. He ain't worth a farthing now to Captain Scratch, for sure and certain he ain't. Or yerself either, Oliver. I mislike to say it, but I don't think ye can see a spirit any better than the rest of us, no matter what hour ye was born."

I raised my eyes and gazed at him. There was such a thunder in my head for a moment that I couldn't hear Captain Scratch counting away the seconds in the cove. A sigh cracked my lips. I felt a great darkness lift from my mind—and a burden, too. I couldn't see ghosts. I didn't want to see ghosts. By thunder, I didn't *believe* in ghosts!

"Strike me ugly," John Ringrose sighed. "That means we're done for. We'll never get our hooks on that plunder."

"Aye," Jack o' Lantern nodded. "There's no way to get a fix on it. It's lost."

"*Forty-seven!*" shouted Captain Scratch. "Do ye hear, boy! *Forty-eight!*"

I was ready to streak it for the cove, but thought I'd have to fight my way out of Jack o' Lantern's grip first. "Let the old fool wait," he said, making a twist in my pigtail. "Tuck in yer shirt. We can't have ye presenting yerself to the captain looking like ye climbed out of a hole. I see ye got them dark stains out of yer shirt. Bucko, I'll have to find ye that genipa tree and teach ye how to eat 'em without making such a mux of it."

When I glanced down I saw for the first time that the spots were gone. I was hugely astonished.

« *117*

"Fifty-three!"

"He won't harm ye, bucko," said Jack o' Lantern. "Not as long as he thinks he needs ye. Hark, now, to what I say. String him along. Get him in the jungle. Then break away and make for the longboat. John and I will be there. We'll make for the ship and maroon the old devil."

He gave me a shove on my way. I broke through the leaves and put off across the sand. And then Captain Scratch saw me, at the count of fifty-nine.

He lowered Jibboom and grinned. I slowed to a walk. I almost stopped. There was such a sudden ferment of thoughts in my head that I almost forgot Jibboom. I glanced over my shoulder toward Jack o' Lantern and Mr. Ringrose hidden in the rim of the cove, and could hardly keep from rushing back. I *knew* where the treasure was buried. Unless I missed my guess, I knew *exactly* where.

Captain Scratch clamped hands on me, like irons, and Jibboom jumped free. "Tried to give me the slip, did ye, lad! Why, I wouldn't harm ye for the Grand Mogul's own treasury! Ha! Be glad I come to fetch ye. We're weighing anchor."

I was proper stunned. "Leaving the island?" I choked.

"Aye! The vaporous gent will keep, and the buried gold, too. The ship is springing leaks so fast we won't have a deck under our feet in many more days. We're going cruising for a new ship, boy! And never ye fret about that slabbering Billy Bombay. Seize me soul, he wouldn't be worth the effort to string him up and jerk him into the arms of the devil. It's yourself I'm looking out for. In the longboat with ye!"

I dug my feet in the sand. How could I leave now? Jibboom leaped up on my shoulder and spat at Captain Scratch. He reared back and laughed, and I said, "I'll go fetch Mr. Ring-rose."

"Blast that jimber-jawed scarecrow. He'd make us thirteen aboard. It's yerself alone I come for, boy. In the boat!"

My mind was racing. "But I saw the ghost," I said, and it was more or less the truth. "Bright as daylight. I can lead you to the very spot, sir."

The lights came up in his eyes. His fingers dug into my arms. "Ye *saw* him, did ye say!"

"All aglow. Oh, he was splendiferous to see," I added. "And I saw him seep right down into his grave."

Captain Scratch jerked an arm to the men waiting at the longboat. "Did ye hear that! The treasure! Fetch up the shovels! This way, this way! Come on, me hearties!"

I stuffed Jibboom into my shirt and led the way. I knew better than to try to make a run for it now. We tracked deeper into the jungle and it must have been almost half an hour when I stopped and pointed at a tree. *"There,"* I said.

Captain Scratch's face fell a cable length. *"There?"* he scowled, for I was pointing to a poisonous manchineel tree, shaggy to the ground and hanging with dwarf apples. The very sight of it almost made my face swell up again as it had my first night on the island.

"There," I nodded. "The ghost lowered himself not three feet from the trunk, sir."

The buccaneers began walking round and round the tree as if it were a tangle of snakes. They knew better than to touch it. Finally Captain Scratch handed Hajji his broken cutlass and told him to start hacking away the branches.

"Me, *effendi?*"

"Aye, ye Red Sea dog. Unless ye want the gift of a pistol ball between your eyes!"

Captain Scratch drew his pistol and Hajji took up the cutlass. He began whacking down the hanging branches, muttering and wailing in his own tongue. In not many hours he would be scalded red and stinging from head to toe. I tried to feel sorry for him, without overdoing it.

Sure of the treasure at last, Captain Scratch lost interest in me. I sat on a rock to watch, calming Jibboom inside my shirt, and then silently faded back into the jungle. Once out of sight, I ran.

Jack o' Lantern and Mr. Ringrose were crouched down in the longboat waiting for me.

"Good lad," Jack o' Lantern smiled. "Let's shove off."

I glanced back over my shoulder. Once Captain Scratch found me missing, he was likely to put Cannibal on my trail—but there was no sight of him. "Wait," I said, gasping for breath. "The treasure. I know where it's buried!"

Jack o' Lantern gazed at me. "Has the heat got ye, bucko?" He shook his head. "There's only one way to find the plunder and that's to dig up this island from one end to the other. If we worked fast, we might finish the job in fifty years."

"Look at my shirt!" I cried. "Those juice spots disappeared like invisible ink. Is there only one genipa tree on the island?"

"Aye. That's all I've found, though they grow common enough on Hispaniola."

I was sure of myself now. "Gentleman Jack had just *come* from Hispaniola when the *Bloody Hand* pulled in here to bury the plunder, sir. Captain Scratch said that all the while he was marking those bearings on his sleeve, he was dipping his quill in a Hispaniola fruit. Using the juice for ink. A disappearing ink without knowing it, I fancy. The same as these genipa spots on my shirt." I paused for breath. "But when he was shot and buried over, the genipa must have been buried, too. *It could have sprouted.* It's been seven years hasn't it?"

Jack o' Lantern's face was aglow with the possibility of it. "Ye think them treasure boxes are waiting in the roots of the genipa tree, do ye?"

"Yes, sir!"

"Strike me ugly!" said John Ringrose.

CHAPTER 16

*Of what befell us, one and all,
and the ghost who
stayed behind*

WHILE CAPTAIN Scratch dug under the manchineel tree we were digging up the genipa tree on the other end of the island. It looked very like a cherry tree, except for the bigness of the fruit hanging from the branches like five-pounder cannonballs.

It wasn't long before we uncovered a skeleton.

"Gentleman Jack—for sure and certain!" Jack o' Lantern gasped.

"Aye," said John Ringrose in awe.

For an instant my knees went limsy again, seeing the old pirate chief with the roots of the tree wound through his bones like serpents. It was a scaresome sight, even in broad daylight.

"John," said Jack o' Lantern. "Hurry back to the boat and

fetch the crew left aboard ship. There's more plunder under our feet than we can tote."

Mr. Ringrose flew off through the jungle. I kept glancing over my shoulder as if Cannibal might pounce on me at any moment.

"Lend a hand, bucko," Jack o' Lantern said—meaning to help him lift out the skeleton. He was busy cutting the roots with his knife. I gulched down my horror of it—and lent a hand.

Before long the corner of an iron chest came into view. We were going at it full chisel when I glanced up and saw Jibboom shoot up on his legs—and spit.

There was Cannibal with his eyes grinning away at me. He didn't see Jack o' Lantern, deeper in the hole on his hands and knees.

"Ha! I catch you, boy! Too bad. Cannibal like you. But Captain say—" and here he ran a finger across his throat. "Ha! Maybe I give you chance. Better run, boy!"

Jack o' Lantern's head rose up from the sandy pit. "Welcome, Fiji friend."

Cannibal's eyes popped. "You dead man!"

"Not quite. Give a hand. Plenty gold!"

"By jingo."

"Ye join us?"

Cannibal seemed almost eager to desert Captain Scratch. "I dig."

The iron chest was so heavy that not even the three of us could lift it out of the ground. Before long John Ringrose returned with Ezra Fly and Big Nose Ned and the others, except for Billy Bombay. Three chests were brought up—the one huge one and two the size of tar kegs.

"Cannibal," said Jack o' Lantern, even before the lids could be broken open, "let's give Captain Scratch a look. Fetch him."

"Capting Scratch?" said John Ringrose, shutting one eye. "Why, it was him that shot Gentleman Jack here. That's what he was ravin' about the night of the dredgies. I told ye that. He ain't entitled to anything, I say."

"But Gentleman Jack is," said Jack o' Lantern. "We all knew him like a brother, didn't we? He's entitled to be proper avenged. I intend to clap the villain out of Captain Scratch so he'll regret his entire pesky life. Fetch him!"

Cannibal set out, having been warned not to let on that Jack o' Lantern was on the island, and the men went at the locks. There was a regular shindy when the big lid was flung back and sunlight itself shot out at us. The chest was heaped and overflowing with gold—Spanish doubloons and French louis d'or and even golden dinars from the Red Sea.

The buccaneers slabbered at the sight of it. They broke open the smaller boxes and feasted their eyes on pearls and rubies and emeralds. They slipped so many rings on their fingers that their seafaring hands were a very blaze of lights. Jack o' Lantern had needed that dazzling plunder to win their loyalty—and he had it to a man.

Captain Scratch broke into the clearing. Clapping eyes on that glitter of gold and jewels, he stopped in his tracks. The eyebrows all but flew off his face. "Seize me soul! So ye found it, boys! Blast your eyes, ye found it when me back was turned!"

He took a step closer and rested a hand on the pistol in his sash. He looked from face to face and his eyes came to rest on me. My heart rose into my throat, despite myself. Jack o' Lantern had snugged himself out of sight.

"Why, it's young Oliver is it?" he snorted. "What kind of jigamaree was ye about—putting us to digging up the wrong tree? But I see your ghosting eyes didn't fail ye, after all. Bless me soul, if that ain't Gentleman Jack himself stretched out there. And look at all them baubles ye lads is sporting—as if I give the order to cut up shares." The anger came up in him hot and sudden. He drew his pistol and took a step backward. "Into the boxes with the stuff, ye greedy vermin! I'll take first pick and half the booty—and give a pistol ball to the first man who says I don't!"

Seeing us all ranged before him he had no one to fear—except Jack o' Lantern, who at that very moment was swinging a branch of iron wood down on his skull.

In no time at all the crew had the heavy treasure box on stout bamboo poles, and we were all making for the cove. Captain Scratch was carried along, alive, but limp as canvas. He would awake with a monstrous headache.

While the treasure was being hauled into the longboat, Jack o' Lantern lifted up a bottom board and handed it to me. "Carve his name on it, bucko. No time to lose. And maybe a word or two fitting the occasion."

Meanwhile he took up a shovel and formed a long mound of earth above the rim of the cove.

I made quick cuts in the wood with my jackknife until it read:

> CAPT. SCRATCH
> *Rest His Timbers*

*   *   *

The moment I was through, Jack o' Lantern took the board and pounded it at one end of the mound—like a headstone. Captain Scratch was already beginning to make snorting sounds where they had stretched him out on the beach. Mr. Ringrose helped himself to the knives and pistols in his sash. Jack o' Lantern gave a signal for all the men to gather around the mound and headstone.

"And don't forget to bow yer heads."

"Is his eyes open yet?" asked Mr. Ringrose, taking a stance at the foot of the mound.

"Fluttering. Make it a fine oration, John, with thunderclaps of fire and brimstone. And the rest of ye remember—ye can't *see* or *hear* the captain. Aye, yer deaf and dumb and blind to him. We'll give the old fox such a fright as will make a lamb out of him."

I stood back from the others with Jibboom in my shirt, and Jack o' Lantern waded into the water and hid himself behind the longboat. The moment Captain Scratch opened his eyes, John Ringrose raised his voice.

"Shipmates," he said. "It's me sad duty to say a few last words over our departed capting and comrade, Harry Scratch. Struck down in the prime of life, he was. There he stood with a fortune at his feet and a coconut tree over his head. One dropped. Aye, an unfortunate act of fate. Here he lies on this lonely island—but not forgotten."

By this time Captain Scratch had raised himself to a sitting position and was wincing under the burden of the knot on his head. He peered at John Ringrose out of one eye. "Ye long-legged sea worm—what are ye bellowing about?"

"Aye, here lies Capting Scratch, rest his timbers," Mr. Ringrose continued. "Oh, I can smell the brimstone risin' up from his grave already. Shed a tear, boys. He's headed in the wrong direction."

Captain Scratch had now staggered to his feet and was trying to focus his eyes. "What's that jabbering! You, John! Ezra Fly! Cannibal!"

Not a head turned.

"Aye, he had a weakness for foul deeds, did Harry Scratch," Mr. Ringrose lamented. "Through no fault of his own, ye might say. He was just born scurvy-hearted and never lived to outgrow it."

By this time Captain Scratch was roaring. "Avast, shipmates! Have ye all gone deaf!"

Our heads remained bowed.

Captain Scratch took a step closer and clapped eyes on the mound and headstone. If he couldn't read, he appeared to recognize his own name.

"Ye fools!" he blustered. "I ain't in me grave, boys! I'm standing right here before ye!"

"Shed a tear, boys—if ye can. Ain't there one tear among us?" asked John Ringrose. "Even if he did do Gentleman Jack most foul and prod his shipmates off the end of a plank—why, there must have been some good in him that we can say to his credit, on this solemn occasion."

Captain Scratch was waving his arms about in a fury. "Look at me, shipmates! Avast! Blast your eyes—can't ye see me!" His gaze fastened on me. "Look at me, boy—"

The very words caught in his throat.

"I can see you," I answered.

The color drained out of his face. His beard began to tremble. "Is it only yourself who can see me?" he asked in a quavering voice. "Is that it? Have I turned ghost?"

"Hardly cold in the ground is our capting, poor Harry Scratch—and already beginning to smolder," John Ringrose sighed. "If he'd treated his fellow cutthroats better he might be goin' to a cooler climate." At this point Mr. Ringrose lifted his eyes to the blue sky. "Aye, here rests his timbers with the fires of Hades roastin' him from below and the noonday sun from above. Let it be a lesson to us all, boys. Aye—and let's shove off."

The buccaneers turned and went for the longboat.

"Wait a bit, maties," said Captain Scratch. "Hold on—"

But the men looked through him as if he were glass.

"Don't leave me, lads. Oh, I done some terrible things—wait. Avast. Can't ye hear what I'm saying? Don't go—"

In no time at all we had piled into the longboat and the skiff. No one looked back. Except me.

Captain Scratch was standing in the noonday sun with his feet rooted in the sand—all the thunder clapped out of him. The wind was blowing his red beard, but the fierceness was gone out of it. Jack o' Lantern climbed up beside me in the stern of the boat, but kept his head low.

"Gentleman Jack is proper avenged," he said. "Aye—Harry Scratch will walk that island thinking he's a ghost, and waiting for the devil to come fetch him. Who knows, boy—he might get picked up in a year or two or five. If the surprisal ain't too much for him—why, he'll be turned as honest as a parson."

Captain Scratch grew smaller and smaller. Even though no one had shed a tear for him he gave us a last, forlorn wave of his hand. Despite myself, I waved back.

128 »

*   *   *

We were six days at sea when the *Bloody Hand* began to sink. The hull was popping new holes by the hour and we had to give up on the pumps. The sea turtles stowed live in the hold were now swimming around in the foc'sle. John Ringrose, who had been elected captain, decided it was time to abandon ship. He wore his scarlet coat and feathered cap and sorely hated to give up his first command.

"Into the boat, lads!" he cried sadly.

Billy Bombay and Hajji were among the first to go for the chests of treasure. When Jack o' Lantern saw that heavy plunder hauled into the longboat, he gave me the eye. "Into the skiff with us, bucko."

Together, we gathered up stalks of bananas and casks of water. The decks were almost awash. We loaded up the rowboat and Captain Ringrose spied the treasure in the long-boat. "Scuttle that deadweight, boys! It's food ye'll be wantin'!"

But the crew ignored him. They shoved off in the overbur-dened longboat, and I helped Jack o' Lantern get the skiff into the water. Captain Ringrose joined us, and not a moment too soon. A great bubble of air billowed through the ship, cough-ing up live turtles. With a final roar the ship went under and the turtles streaked it in every direction.

The *Bloody Hand* was no more.

The longboat, burdened to the gunwales with men and plun-der, stood a pistol shot away on the rising sea.

"Well, they've got a ton of gold aboard," said Jack o' Lantern, pulling on the oars. "But the fools won't find it overly appetiz-ing when they get hungry."

"She's swamping already," said Captain Ringrose. He stood in the rowboat, and gave a shout through his hands.

"Scuttle that deadweight, I tell ye! Ye'll go under!"

But the buccaneers wouldn't give up so much as a doubloon. They pushed through the chop of the sea, as if to leave us behind.

Jack o' Lantern began to chuckle. "Looks like they don't want to share-out with us."

With every stroke of the oars, the longboat dipped deeper into the brine. The oars were going lickety-cut when before our very eyes the longboat swamped and sank—gold and all.

Captain Ringrose's jaw fell. "Strike me ugly," he said. "It's enough to cure a man of keepin' ignorant company."

We turned about to look for survivors. There was only one. Cannibal could swim. We fetched him aboard.

We were four men and a cat. A turtle boat picked us up some days later. Jibboom and I were more than two months getting home, traveling by foot and by sea, and it was a spring day when we walked through the door of the Harpooner's Inn. Aunt Katy almost dropped a full pot of cod chowder on old Mr. Wicks, the cooper. "Dearlove," she sighed, and fainted. A man caught her in midair.

It was my father.

He looked me over with his seafaring eyes, and seemed hugely surprised. And pleased at what he saw. I was brown as a nut from the southern sun.

A smile now lurked in a corner of his eye. "Tarnation!" he said. "Help me with this plaguey woman."

"Aye, sir," I said.

"Thee has grown a head taller, boy."

"Yes, sir." We got Aunt Katy into a chair and she began coming around.

He straightened. "I've been up and down the coast inquiring after thee, son." He cleared his throat, for it seemed as choked up as my own. "Where is it thee has been?"

"At sea," I answered, and hung my briny cap on a hook beside my father's.